# THE SAVOY

### AND OTHER STORIES

## STEPHEN MURPHY

BLACK GATE
MEDIA

Published by Blackgate Media
(a Blackgate Services Ltd imprint)

FIRST EDITION

ISBN 978-1-9996630-4-9 (paperback)
ISBN 978-1-9996630-3-2 (ebook)

*For Juliet*

# CONTENTS

# WEIGHT

Michael looks out the window of the workshop to see old Will sitting with his back to him, staring out into an empty street. Even though he cannot see his face, he knows Will must be having a bad day. He isn't working. And if he isn't working, he is thinking. Usually, that means thinking about Alice. As Michael sighs, the window clouds. He puts on his jacket, grabs two beers from the fridge and goes outside to sit with his boss, his old friend.

Michael pulls up an old crate and sits next to Will. The old man continues to stare out into the empty street on this brisk, autumn early morning. He hands him a beer, and both take a gulp.

"Bit early for lager."

"Yeah."

The small village of Eschol is bathed in golden hues. The clouds in the hills beyond the valley warn of wet possibilities. Both men sit silently. Michael swallows more beer. He holds up the half-empty bottle in the light. He positions the sun behind the glass, refracting rainbows on his own face. He waits. Will looks over.

"How heavy do you think this bottle of beer is?" Will looks at him puzzled but says nothing and lets Michael continue. "Eight ounces? two hundred grams?"

"If you're gonna give the half-full, half-empty speech, don't bother."

Michael smiles. "The exact weight doesn't matter. It's how long I hold on to it for." Michael pauses, awaiting a response. Will blinks. "If I sit here for a minute, it's fine. If I sit here and try to hold this bottle aloft for hour upon hour, it will become heavy. A burden. Too much for me to hold on to. It will start to hurt. It will stop me from doing other things."

Will is listening but giving nothing away.

"If I put down the bottle and release my grip..." Michael puts the glass bottle back down on the table. There is a moment as Michael waits to let Will answer.

"Someone might take the bottle away."

"Or someone else might fill it back up or even give you another" Will looks back up to the sky. Both men sit quietly. A breeze picks up. The clouds seem to darken. Will looks at his beer bottle. He misses her still. Michael is probably right, Jayne is a wonderful woman, but he's not ready. Not yet.

"There's gonna be a storm. Let's get this stuff inside."

# THE END

It has been two hard years, and still Anna had yet to finish that difficult second novel.

Her first, entitled The End, was "a masterpiece in taut story-telling" and "a confident debut." Or so the *Middlewich Gazette* and the *Bishop Fold Chronicle* had said. Anna's publisher was getting impatient, but she had managed to appease her with what she said was a "finished" children's story. Although at first Hilary was taken aback that Anna was taking a whole new direction, and then worried that it was instead of the second novel, she was eventually reassured that this was something extra. Anna said she just needed to try it out on the intended audience first to check a few things and she and Hilary agreed on a deadline of next Tuesday.

Anna had two sisters, Lauren and Kiera. Lauren wasn't really a sister, but a step-sister. She was ten years her junior and lived in Perth with her estranged dad. Kiera was her sensible older birth sister by four years. Kiera lived with her own six-year-old daughter, Chloe, in a flat in a suburb of Harsham. She was a nurse, divorced from that pig Larry, but seeing a much-too-young beau called Mav. He was a musician, and that was all that needed to be said about him. Besides, it didn't matter because Anna had made sure it was just going to be her sister and Chloe in when she called round. She had warned Kiera about her intentions and that she wanted Chloe to listen to her story. She would be there on Sunday afternoon at 2pm for tea, biscuits, and to be left alone with the girl and her book.

When Anna arrived at her sister's flat, Chloe was already excited to see the new book her auntie Anna had for her. Even before she managed to get through the door, Chloe was full of questions.

"Can I see it?"

"In a minute. Let your auntie Anna get in the house first." Kiera turned to Anna. "Tea?"

"Please."

"I've never had a book written for me before," bubbled Chloe.

Anna scowled and mumbled under her breath to her sister. "For her?"

Kiera shrugged. "First I've heard of it."

Anna took off her jacket and hung it in the hallway. She made her way to the sitting room, closely followed by a skipping Chloe, as Kiera went to the kitchen.

"What's it called? Who's in it? Am I in it? Can I draw the cover picture?"

*Five-year-olds*, thought Anna. *They are just plain annoying.*

"Sit down, calm down, and I will show it to you."

Still smiling, Chloe jumped onto the sofa and held out her hands. Anna took the rucksack from her shoulder and sat beside her. She unzipped the bag and pulled out a manuscript of around forty typed white A4 pieces of paper. Chloe looked very disappointed.

"Where's the book?"

"This is the book. It hasn't been published yet. So there is no cover, no pictures yet."

Chloe looked nonplussed. "I'll draw them for you."

"That's okay. My publisher already has a graphic artist in mind."

Once again, Chloe was disappointed. Her bottom lip started to protrude.

"Look, do you want to hear the story or not?"

Chloe nodded. Kiera entered with a tray of cups, teapot and a plate of Hobnobs. She poured the tea, kissed Chloe on the head and started to leave.

"I'll leave you to it. I've got lots of ironing to do."

Anna placed her rucksack on the floor and made herself comfortable. As she reclined on the sofa, Chloe snuggled up to her.

"Leave me room to be able to turn the pages."

"Sorry." Chloe hugged a cushion instead. She stared at her auntie and wondered how someone so pretty could be so silly, and then Anna started to read her story aloud to the little girl.

Kiera was getting through a large pile of ironing and had noticed her sister had stopped reading around fifteen minutes ago. She could hear them both chatting and decided to take a break and join them. As she walked into the sitting room, the two of them were at the coffee table doing a jigsaw together. Anna seemed less grumpy than usual, but her daughter was much too quiet.

"Finished?"

"Yes."

"Did you like it?"

Chloe nodded slowly. Her face said otherwise. Kiera didn't press her on it, but Anna picked up on it straightaway.

"Did you like the main character?"

Chloe shrugged her shoulders. Anna looked to her sister for help.

"What did you like about it, darling?" Kiera sat next to her and started to join in doing the jigsaw puzzle.

"I suppose I like the funny ones."

"Which funny ones?" interjected Anna, rather too quickly.

"Mr. Enk and his friend the Dondor. I like them." Thinking about this, Chloe suddenly seemed to come to life, and she took the characters and made them her own with her imagination. "I liked that they lived in the land of Pinty Pinty because that's what Grandad used to call his walking stick, and the cloud people were funny because they had no legs, and the Dondor was like an elephant all big and silly, and... err, that's it."

"That sounds great, sweetheart." Kiera turned to her sister. "Positive?"

"Yeah, great, except half of that she made up." Anna turned to Chloe. "What about the main character? Sugar? Do you remember her? She was the narrator. The pretty girl who didn't like silly people."

"I didn't like her."

"What? She's the protagonist, the storyteller!"

Chloe ignored her aunt and tried doing some of the jigsaw.

"I'll make another cup of tea," said Kiera. "Can I read it?"

"Help yourself."

Kiera got up and went back to the kitchen with the

manuscript and left the other two sulking in the sitting room.

Anna and Chloe sat quietly doing the jigsaw puzzle as Kiera read the story. As she reached the final page and turned it over, a broad knowing smile stretched across her face.

"I've got the last piece, Chloe." Anna went to put in the last tile of the puzzle, but it was a cheap bargain, second-hand effort that Kiera hand bought from a charity shop, and it was reluctant to go in properly.

"It's the wrong bit, Auntie Anna."

"No, it's the right piece, it just doesn't fit correctly." She tried to force it in and then bashed it with her palm.

When it was time to go, Anna kissed her sister on the cheek, put on her jacket and left.

Kiera went back inside after shutting the door and sat with Chloe, who was watching a cartoon.

"Why won't Auntie Anna let me draw her a picture for her book? I'm good at drawing."

"Yes, you are." Another pause with just the sound of the cartoon from the TV.

"Why does Auntie Anna write books, Mummy?"

Smiling, Kiera said, "I guess it's because she is a story-teller, a narrator."

"I'm going to write a book about Mr Enk and the Dondor. And draw the pictures."

Kiera wrapped her arms around her daughter and they watched the cartoon together.

# PROSOPAGNOSIA

Pearl opens her eyes. Her head hurts. Her vision is blurred. She looks around her. She is in bed, but not hers. She looks to her left; a window with a lovely view of a concrete wall. She turns, a nurse in uniform is fussing around, busy, until she noticed Pearl's eyes have opened.

"Hello, you. How are you feeling?"

"Terrible."

"I'm not surprised."

Pearl leans on her arm and tries to sit-up.

"Hang on, let me help." The nurse places the clipboard she is holding down and grasps Pearl's arm and supports her. She leans her forward and puts an extra pillow behind her, then rests her back against it. "Better?"

"Yes, thanks."

"Do you want anything before I go get the doctor?"

"Just some water, please?"

The nurse fills a plastic beaker with some tepid tap water and hands it to Pearl.

"Back in five. She's only on the next ward."

Pearl nods and sips the drink. It tastes like wet dust. She looks at the drip in her arm, then under the blanket. A thick bandage is wrapped around her middle. She instinctively touches the bit that hurts and makes it hurt some more. She pulls the cover back up and starts to remember the loud bang, the searing pain, like fire in her middle. The doctor enters.

"Miss Baggs, I'm Doctor Malik. Glad to see you awake. Do you know why you're here?"

"I got shot."

"Yes, you did. The bullet went straight through your right kidney and out the other side. Lucky for you, you have two, and I was able to stop the bleeding."

Direct and to the point, thought Pearl.

"It's been a bit of a struggle keeping those annoying policemen from harassing you, but we coped, didn't we, June?"

The nurse looks at the doctor and nods, but the doctor carries on looking at Pearl.

"Once word gets out that you're alive and kicking, they will be in here like a flash asking you lots of questions."

She walks over to the window and looks out at nothing.

"Do you think you're up to it?"

She doesn't turn around to look for an answer, or even wait for one.

"Wasn't just you shot, you see. Four people were. And they're not in the hospital."

Pearl looks at the nurse, who looks to the floor. The doctor snaps out of it and starts for the door.

"Right, off on my rounds. Chin up, Miss Baggs."

And off she goes. Pearl looks at the door until it shuts behind the doctor.

"If you need me, just press the button," says the nurse. "Get some more rest before they do come."

Pearl is unsure how long she was out again, but the pain in her head has eased off a little. No sign of the nurse or Doctor Malik. But there is a woman, sat in the visitor's chair at the far end of the room. In her sixties, at a guess, but quite chic for her age.

*I wonder if I know her*, thinks Pearl. When she sees Pearl's eyes are open, the woman looks up from her magazine and smiles.

"I'm sorry I missed you the first time you woke up. I had to go home to feed the dog and take her out."

"That's okay."

The woman moves over to the side of the bed. "I'm your mum, love."

Pearl nods. "I thought you might be."

"The doctor said you're gonna be okay, but it will take a while to heal and you have to take it easy. Said you were lucky."

"I don't feel lucky."

"No, I suppose not, but the others..." She seems to think better of what she was going to say and changes tack. "June is lovely, isn't she?"

"Who?"

"The nurse, June."

"Oh, yes, she seems nice."

"I got you a magazine." She goes back to the chair and picks up the magazine she was reading and places it on the end of Pearl's bed. "It's not very good."

"Thanks, anyway."

"Oh, I nearly forgot!" She quickly returns to the chair and picks up a handbag that was hung on the arm. She fumbles around inside, looking for something.

"I've brought your photographs from your purse. Here." She passes a handful of tatty old printed photographs to Pearl. The first one is a picture of the woman in front of her. Pearl turns the photograph over and on the other side it says, "Mum". She looks up and Mum smiles again. Not a very happy smile, more a knowing smile from experience. The next picture is of a man who looks a similar age to Mum. On the flip-side, it says "Dad" with the word "died" in brackets after it in green ink. The next is a woman around Pearl's own age with bright red curly hair. She seems to be called "Megan (friend, best)". The last is a twenty-something male with the same lank straight hair as Pearl. His states "Ray (little brother)".

"Thanks, Mum." Pearl tries out this last word to see how it feels. The woman brightens at hearing it.

"I fancy a coffee. Want one, darling? I'll go down to canteen and get us one." She closes her handbag and goes to exit. As she reaches for the handle, the door opens and in comes a hospital porter.

"Don't mind me. Just off to get coffee" And with that, she departs. The porter watches her go and closes the door behind him. He turns to face Pearl and stands still and stares.

"You okay?" says Pearl. He looks confused.

"Are you?" he replies. He still hasn't moved from the end of the bed. Pearl nods and smiles. Still looking perplexed, he smiles back. Pearl makes that "and?" look and shrugs her shoulders. "I've done that thing where you go into a room and as soon as you are in there, you forgot what you came in for," says the porter.

"Ah, I see. Try going out and coming back in again."

"I might." There is another short, awkward silence before the porter speaks again. "Have we met before?"

*Ah,* thinks Pearl. *We either have met before, and he thinks I'm being rude, or he is trying to chat me up. Due to my current state and look, it is probably the former.* She decides to explain, her practiced speech for those that feel hurt because she doesn't recognise them.

"Possibly, but I wouldn't know."

He furrows his brow and purses his lips as a way of saying, "please tell," so Pearl continues.

"I have prosopagnosia." Her brow becomes even more creased. "I don't recognise faces. Doesn't matter how many times we've met. If you don't introduce yourself, I won't know who you are. I can guess or fake it sometimes, but the lady who just left is my mum, and she had to remind me who she was."

"Really?"

"Really. So have we met?" It seems to take a moment for it all to sink in.

"Er, no, no."

"So don't feel bad about forgetting what you came in for. I forget my own mum."

"Wow." *He seems to like what he hears,* she thinks. He moves around the bed and looks like he is about to say something else when the door suddenly opens and Mum comes back in holding two coffees, accompanied by two middle-aged white men in bad suits. One holds the door open for her.

"The police want to talk to you, Pearl."

Pearl looks at the one who opened the door for her mum. He seems to take a step back, and the other one steps forward. He gestures with his hand to his colleague, while still looking at Pearl.

"This is Detective Saunders, and I'm DS Philips. I hope you're feeling better, Miss Baggs, as we need to talk to you."

"Take a seat." She looks around to see where they could sit and notices the porter has gone.

"That's okay, Miss. We'll stand." Her mum places the coffee on the bedside table and takes the only seat in the room to sip her own coffee. Detective Saunders pulls out a notepad and pencil, and Detective Sergeant Philips continues to speak.

"I am sure you understand why we're here?"

Pearl nods, and her mum interjects. "I've already told them you won't be able to help."

"Yes, thank you, Mrs. Baggs, but we need to hear it from your daughter. Your mother informs us that you have some sort of condition?"

"And you don't believe her."

"It's not that, Miss. It just seems..."

"Unbelievable?"

"Her neurologist is Doctor Williams. Just ask him," says Pearl's mum.

"We will," continues Philips. "So you can't remember what the man who shot you looked like?"

"It's not that I can't remember. I'm unable to process faces. I can't recognise them."

"Well, what was he wearing?"

"A blue two piece, single-breasted suit, white shirt, black shoes, and a black skinny tie." Detective Saunders quickly starts to scribble the description.

"He was a man. Errr, he had short, dark hair."

"Okay, good. How tall?"

"A shade under six feet, and quite thick set. Not fat.

Looked like he worked out. I was looking through the glass of the little side office they have in the bank. The manager had left me there to sign some papers. I'd just done them when the two men burst in."

"Two men?" This seems like news to Philips, and he glances over at Saunders before returning to Pearl.

"You didn't know there were two?"

"Miss Baggs, you are our only witness. You were the only customer as they were just closing up, and as you know, the two bank clerks and the manager were shot dead."

"It was the second man."

"The second man?"

"He killed the bank staff."

"And what did he look like?"

"A brown two-piece suit, white shirt collar, and had his head shaved to the skin. That's all I could see of him. He had his back to me when he...well, when he shot those poor people."

"And what was your assailant doing at this time?"

"He was by the front door. Watching, I guess. But when his partner started firing, he must have heard me yelp."

"Oh, Pearl." Her mum holds her hand to her face.

"I tried to duck, but it was too late. He had already seen me. He came over to the window and looked in to see me on the floor. He shouted something over to his friend, but I didn't quite hear what it was, and then he just seem to stand there."

"And what was his partner doing at this time?"

"Like I said, I was on the floor and terrified at this point."

"I understand."

"It seemed to be an age until I heard the other one shout at the one at the door to get on with it. That's when I heard the door open. I looked up, looked him straight in the eyes, but he seemed to hesitate, like he didn't want to shoot. So I stood up. I started moving towards him and he lowered his pistol. He let me go past him. I saw the door and made a dash for it and heard the other man shout 'Do it!' There was a huge bang. Then all I remember is waking up in the hospital." Recalling the events makes her side hurt. She presses the button for the nurse and winces in pain.

"Right, that's enough," says her mum as she bolts out of the chair, pushing past Saunders and over to Pearl's bedside.

"You've been very helpful, Miss Baggs. We will need to talk to you again at some—" Before he finishes his sentence, the nurse bursts in and asks them to leave as well. They nod out of respect and bid farewell. Pearl takes one more painkiller and falls back asleep.

"You should have shot her first time round," Dawson spits. Meeks just sits on the motel bed and says nothing. Dawson continues to pack the money into a brown duffle bag.

"Can't even follow simple instructions. No witnesses, we said. You don't need masks if you take out the CCTV and anyone in there."

"I know."

"Looked you right in the face."

"I shot her, didn't I?"

"Yeah, but we had to get out of there. Didn't have time to check if she was dead, did we?"

"It's just..."

"Just what?"

"She wasn't afraid. When I pointed the gun at her, she didn't seem afraid. Walked at me."

"You better get it together, lad. You need to finish the job."

"What?"

"That's right. The nearest emergency hospital to the bank is St. Bartholomew's. That's where she'll be. And you need to get in there and do what you should have done in the first place."

"The pigs will be everywhere."

"They're useless. Takes them ages to know what happened. Get out of the suit, into the jeans and T-shirt and get in the car. I'll drive." Dawson throws the clothes at Meeks. "In and out. Got it?"

Meeks nods.

The beat up Mondeo pulls up in a short-stay parking zone right outside the critical care unit. Meeks checks his pistol and puts it inside his belt.

"You know what to do?" says Dawson.

"Yes."

"Do we need to go over it again?"

Meeks doesn't answer. He opens the passenger side door.

"Thirty minutes then I'm gone...with or without you."

Meeks slams the door shut and makes his way over to the entrance.

Inside, he looks at the map. Critical care wards are up a floor in the yellow zone. He walks on. Before going to the ward, he seems to be looking for something else, somewhere else. He notices a sign saying maintenance. He follows that to a door labelled G2. He looks left and right and enters. After five minutes or so, he comes back out dressed in a hospital porter's uniform. He closes the door and continues to the critical care wards. He takes the stairs rather than the lift and walks along the corridors to the yellow zone. There are four wards here. Two are critical care. He sees an empty wheelchair parked outside a disabled toilet and pushes it to the first care ward door. The lock is on. Meeks presses the buzzer and after a moment, a nurse comes over.

"I was asked to drop this off."

"For who?"

"I didn't ask."

The nurse sighs, exasperated at his incompetence, and buzzes him in. "Put it over by the waiting area until I find out who it's for."

Meeks nods and starts to push it down the corridor. As the nurse enters the office, he turns and looks at the patient notice board. No one with a bullet wound or anything similar. As he pushes the wheelchair back out the door, the nurse comes out of the office, sees him and shouts after him.

"You must have the wrong ward. No one here ordered a wheelchair."

"I know. Thanks," shouts Meeks without turning and goes to the next ward.

He follows the same routine, although it takes a little longer for someone to answer the door, but a nurse lets him in again. He checks the board. Room Seven, Baggs - body trauma. He leaves the wheelchair where the nurse asks him to and goes to get a glass of water from the cooler and waits for her to leave. When she disappears into a patient's room, he makes his way to Room Seven.

Meeks hesitates, checks his gun in the back of his belt and turns the handle. As he opens the door, a woman comes bursting out.

"Don't mind me. Just off to get coffee."

He watches her go down the corridor and, keeping his back to the room, enters and closes the door behind him. Meeks turns to face the bed and stands still and stares.

"You okay?" says the woman in the bed. Again, she is not scared. She is calm. She is looking straight at him. She seems to be fine.

"Are you?" Meeks still hasn't moved from the end of the bed. The woman nods and smiles. Still perplexed at what she is playing at, he follows along and smiles back.

*She doesn't recognise me in the porter's uniform*, thinks Meeks. She seems to be waiting for a reply.

"I've done that thing where you go into a room and as soon as you are in there you forgot what you came in for," he says.

"Ah, I see. Try going out and coming back in again."

"I might" There is another short awkward silence. Meeks decides to test her. "Have we met before?"

"Ah. Possibly, but I wouldn't know. I have prosopagnosia." Meeks listens, amazed. "I don't recognise faces. Doesn't matter how many times we've met. if you don't introduce yourself, I won't know who you are. I can guess, or fake it sometimes, but the lady who just left is my mum, and she had to remind me who she was."

"Really?"

"Really. So have we met?" It starts to dawn on Meeks how goddamn lucky he is. The cold gun in his back reminds him why he's here. *But now*, he thinks, *the plan has changed*.

"Er, no, no."

"So don't feel bad about forgetting what you came in for. I forget my own mum."

"Wow." Meeks smiles. He really can't believe his luck. He moves forward and is about to ask her what happened to her when the door suddenly opens and the mum comes back in holding two coffees, accompanied by two men.

"The police want to talk to you, Pearl."

*Time to leave*, thinks Meeks. He slips out of the door and out into the waiting car to tell Dawson their good luck. *I doubt he'll believe me*, thinks Meeks.

# WARM-UP MAN

*S*o many old people. Well, pensioners and a group of students. The non-income brigade. This is supposed to be a commercial channel. Who's this programme aimed at? How are you supposed to get advertisers for a programme targeted at the lowest-income bracket? What are you going to sell them? Funeral care plans and debt consolidation, probably. These daytime audiences are the worst. Look at them. How am I supposed to make these people laugh? Half of them I'll have to repeat the lines to because they didn't hear it the first time, and the others will think they're funnier than me. Actually, some of these kids probably will be.

Morris Milligan, sixty-two years old, smooths down his hair in the studio wings. Warm-up man, comedian, and entertainer. He thought by changing his surname from Smith to Milligan, it would give him comedy gravitas, but it didn't make him funnier. Forty years in the biz. He had a slot on a prime-time Saturday entertainment show in the early eighties. He came on just before the man who hit himself in the face with a metal tray to the tune of the *William Tell Overture*, just after the dancing minstrel troop. Light entertainment in its heyday. He did six of the twelve episodes in the summer of '82. Twenty something million people tuning in to watch. Wholesome family viewing. Now this.

*Looking at this lot, I might be able to do some of the material I was doing back in the seventies and eighties. I could even do some of my funny voices. My Indian Dentist used to go down a storm back then. Not so much now. Bloody PC rubbish. The grey brigade would enjoy it, maybe not so the students. The 'woke' generation. I'd be all over social media and not in a good way. I should have worn my blue suit. The leather jacket and blue jeans might be a bit too much for the old dears.*

The audience of around eighty people files in and takes their seats, ready for the show. Clearly, some have never seen a television studio before and find the whole experience fascinating. A couple of older gentlemen in the front row seem rather annoyed that cameras and people operating them will be in the way of the quiz show. They seem to be forgetting the whole purpose of the event, which is a television show. Some of the teenagers in the back row look bored out of their minds.

*Great. Go make the angry mob laugh, Morris. What's the point of having a warm-up comedian for a quiz show based on Scrabble? It's not as if they have to laugh during the show as it isn't funny. Pointless. God knows how Derek does this twice a day, four times a week, to these audiences? He better not be ill for too long. I'm not sure I can handle this for more than a week. Not as if I'm being paid double, either. They just pulled me off my usual job to do this. Got that camp Justin in to do my slot. Why he couldn't just come in for Derek, I don't know? Guess his innuendo-ridden drivel wouldn't sit too well with the wrinklies.*

The floor manager introduces himself to the audience and goes through some house rules. He explains what to do in case of fire, when to clap, and not to talk when the red light is on. He then explains that he will bring out contestants and then the presenter, Mr. Big Ears himself, Lance Heller, and there is an audible intake of breath from the older members of the audience and a continued vow of silence from the younger ones. Then he introduces the warm-up guy, to give them a clue of what to do he starts clapping first and takes two steps back, and on comes Morris Milligan dressed like Top Gun's grandad.

"Thank you, thank you. Ladies and gentlemen, teachers, students, and that guy there..." Slight chuckle from who must be that guy's wife. "Welcome to the first recording of the day of your favourite daytime quiz show...Word-up!" *No applause. Just continue.*

"Look at you lovely people. Anyone been here before?" Three people in the second row put their hands in the air. Morris goes over to the first, a woman with a glass eye, wearing a jumper with cats on. "What's your name, love?"

"Maureen."

"How many times have you been before, Maureen?"

"This is my thirty-seventh." Spontaneous applause of approval.

"I knew that, didn't I, Maureen?" Maureen giggles and makes an "oh you" gesture with her hand.

"Because I saw you on the way in, and you told me that this was your thirty-seventh time."

"I'm eighty-four." An *awwww* followed by more applause.

"Like cats, I see. Are you one of those crazy cat ladies, Maureen?" Morris makes a spinning finger gesture next to his temple and rolls his eyes. A gentle murmur. *Move on.*

"Lots of young people at the back there." Morris waves as if they are a great distance away.

"You lot okay, are you?"

"Yes," replies the teacher and one girl, who is sat next to the teacher. Nothing from the other fourteen. Morris tries again, but louder this time.

"I said all right, are you?" There is a better response, but still not much to write home about. Morris makes his way up the stairs, closer to the teenagers. He sees one young woman in glasses wearing a bright red hoodie that is way too big for her coming all the way down to her knees, even as she's sat down.

"What's your name, sweetheart?"

"Amber, Amber Green."

"Amber Green, dressed in red. Proper little traffic light you, aren't you, love?" Her two nearest friends let out an embarrassed snigger. Morris is unsure whether they laughed at or with him. He is let off the hook by Stevie, the floor manager, announcing Lance Heller onto the studio floor. All, including Morris, turn and clap.

A middle-aged man with far too much fake tan and hair-spray strides out dressed in an immaculate blue suit.

Glad I didn't wear my blue suit, thinks Morris. Morris hears an old lady in a raincoat say "He's very handsome." Then at almost the same time one of the kids to his right exclaims "What a nonce!" Morris smiles.

"Nice to see you all. If anyone would like a photograph, I already have some prepared. Just ask Stevie, and he can arrange it for you. Now I must go to work." He turns towards the set and mumbles something into his microphone as he turns his back to the clapping audience.

"Mr Lance Heller, ladies and gentlemen," says Morris. "Been doing the show for nearly twenty-five years. And still can't spell."

"Two-minutes people!" shouts Stevie from behind the cameras, seemingly to no one in particular.

"Right, everyone. As soon as that red light goes on, we all have to be quiet, even me. That is, unless Stevie asks. He'll tell you when to clap," Morris looks over at the students, "and cheer."

"One minute!"

Morris takes his place just off camera, to the side of the audience near Stevie.

"Ten seconds. Eight, seven, six, five, four." Stevie then holds up three fingers, then two, then one. The red light comes on, and he starts to clap vigorously above his head. Morris joins in. The crowd soon follows. Morris lets out a whoop and gestures for the students to do the same, and to his surprise, a couple of the lads do. After thirty seconds of continuous hooting and slapping of hands, Stevie halts and holds up two thumbs instead. The audience stops, and Lance Heller begins his introduction to the camera. Morris looks at his hands, red from clapping.

*For three years, I've done the* Saturday Night Love Show. *Those audiences know how to have a good time. They open the bars an hour before. I can do some of the good material, maybe even a bit risqué stuff. This is just to keep talking to keep them awake. To keep me awake. Four or five stops, one or two quips, that's all I need from now on. Then do it all again this afternoon. Derek better just have a cold. A paracetamol and a nap and he'll be right as rain, and I can go back to comedy. Okay, not real comedy, but at least I get to tell a few jokes. Maybe even get some laughs. I could have done both. I don't mind not being paid extra as long as that flouncy idiot Justin doesn't get my job.*

∼

The show finishes its recording. Morris does a final thank you. Stevie is asked about photographs but doesn't have any takers when they realise they have to pay £10 for one. The audience files out. Another one over, break for lunch.

"Better than the *Love Show,* Morris?" asks Julie, one of the camera operators who works both shows. She already knows the answer and doesn't even wait for a response, but chuckles to herself as Morris walks away.

On his way to the canteen, Morris switches his phone back on from silent, and it instantly rings in his hand. The read out says it is "The Thief" calling.

"Morris?"

"What?"

"How's the new gig?"

"Dull. You're the worst agent in the world."

"Now, now, Morris, you said you wanted more warm-up work."

"On prime-time shows, not this coffin-dodging drivel."

"They're your demographic these days, lovey."

"Well, I could at least get paid for it."

"You will. Well, you will if Derek is off more than a week, that is."

"How is the old git?"

"Very poorly, so your luck might be in."

"Great. I'll do the *Love Show* as well. Tell Justin he can go back to his clubs."

"We've been through this before, Morris. Justin needs some exposure."

"He can do that down the park with the rest of his kind." Morris drops his voice as he says this last remark, as he knows deep down his homophobic comments are wrong.

"You need to be careful, darling. I spoke to the producer of *Love Show* this morning, and he really likes Justin."

"I bet he does."

"I may have other work for you. How do you fancy an advert?"

"Go on."

"It's for a 'cheeky grandpa type' for a well-known breakfast cereal. And I thought of you. Well, actually I thought of Derek, but he's poorly, so then I thought of you."

"Thanks."

"Good money. If you don't mess it up, it could lead to more commercial work."

"I'm not an actor."

"You don't have to act. Have you ever seen a TV advertisement? All you have to do is be cheeky and old."

Morris arrives at the canteen. While still talking to his agent, he orders cheese and onion pie and chips, and a cup of tea.

"It's perfect timing, Morris. One door closes, another opens."

"I like working on the *Love Show*."

"Well, they like Justin now, so you need to move on. This will open up a whole new chapter for you, my love. I can feel it. Call you next week when Derek is hopefully back, and we'll arrange it all. Bye for now!"

The call ends. Morris sits and looks at his soggy chips and insipid, dry pie. Maybe it will be a new beginning. Perhaps he could get more acting work. Maybe even a sitcom or even a serious role. He thinks of the comedians who go on to do serious work to great acclaim, win awards. He's getting ahead of himself.

Back in the studio and the next audience is coming in. It could be the same group of people as the last show, pensioners near the front, students at the back, even Maureen is back for her thirty-eighth time. Stevie the floor manager does his usual spiel and on comes Morris.

"Thank you, thank you. Ladies and gentlemen, teachers, students, and that guy there..."

The whole front row laughs, and even a couple of the students smile. Morris goes over to a man in a flat cap.

"What did you have for your breakfast this morning, sir?"

# LAURA

*This dust is wreaking havoc with my asthma*, thinks Anya as she opens another old box from her dad's bedroom, labelled 'Photographs (family)' in Bengali. It has been two weeks since the funeral. She and her brother Talin couldn't face going through his belongings until now. They have agreed to meet up at their dad's flat and do it together, just the two of them.

They had done the same thing, but with Dad, three years ago when Mum died. It was hard enough back then because Dad wanted to keep most things. Ayna had to persuade him to let her take Mum's clothes down to the charity shop. Looks like he managed to hide a few things from her back then. She has already found two pairs of shoes, a hat and bed socks that were Mum's in a box under his bed.

"Here's a photograph of Bishwajit." Talin is looking through an album and finds one of the family dog from when they were both kids.

"We'll look through them later. Can we just sort through the things that need to go, not keep?"

Talin does as his big sister says and proceeds to gather shirts and jackets from the wardrobe and place them in bin liners.

"I might keep this shirt with the Cuban cigars on it."

Talin holds the Hawaiian-style shirt up for his sister to see.

"Looks like it hasn't been worn."

Talin holds it up against his chest to check the fit. "I can see why." He shrugs his shoulders and puts the shirt in the bin liner with the rest.

"We should check under the mattress, sis?"

"Why?"

"Don't old people keep their money under there instead of in banks?"

"Dad didn't have any money."

"Not in the bank he didn't."

Talin raises his eyebrows as if to prove a point. Anya shakes her head.

"Have a look then. Whatever is there you can keep."

"Yes, mate."

He leaves the wardrobe half-finished and proceeds to look under his father's mattress. He lifts one corner up, then the other. Then decides to lift the whole thing off and place it to one side of the bedroom.

"Nothing."

"Why you think Dad was hoarding thousands, I have no idea. His train pension was just about enough to live on."

"Yeah, but he liked to play cards with his mates, didn't he? Could have won massive stacks."

"You're an idiot. Go and look through his records and DVDs and see if there is anything you want there. I'll finish the bedroom off."

"Good thinking, sis."

"And take a bin liner and put the ones you don't want in that."

"On it."

Her teenage brother grabs a black bag and goes next door. Anya closes the box with various jigsaw puzzles in and writes *charity shop* on the top of it, before placing it in the hallway.

She puts the rest of his clothes in bags, as the sound of Nat King Cole comes through the wall. Talin has found Dad's old records. Her brother shouts through from the other room.

"Sunday mornings, sis!"

She remembers and smiles. She pauses a moment in her memory of summer weekends spent dancing with her dad as they made breakfast for her mum and little brother. She looks back into the wardrobe. Just two jackets left. The first is a tweed sports number that her dad used to wear for church. She contemplates keeping it, but her practical side gets the best of her sentimental one, and it goes with the others in the bin liners.

The last item in the wardrobe is her dad's old brown overall jacket. He would wear this when he fixed things or pottered around in the shed back in the family garden. Still has a half-chewed pencil in the top pocket. She holds it up on its hanger and looks at the white paint splashes on the sleeves. The dark hazel-coloured stain on the collar. She sniffs it; still a faint odour of creosote. The tag on the inside has been removed and in black marker is *DC*, her dad's initials. Better check the other pockets.

The left side has a flat-headed screwdriver and tape measure in it. The right-side has a photograph. She pulls it out to have a look at it. It is a picture of a beautiful young white woman on it. The photo is old and tatty, the edges worn away, the sheen cracked and it has obviously been folded-up for a long while, as the image is fractured down the middle. She turns the photo over. On the back is a hand-written message.

*From your ever loving girl, Laura xx*

*Who the hell was Laura?* thinks Anya, *and why is there a picture of her in Dad's pocket?*

Otis Redding starts to sing next door.

"Are you sorting them out or just deejaying?" shouts Anya.

Talin doesn't answer, but the music becomes louder. Anya takes another look at the photograph, then puts it in her pocket.

It's been about a week since Anya and her little brother dropped off various items at the local cancer research charity shop. Talin is coming round to her place with the three boxes of photographs they had found, to look through them and sort out. When they had arranged it, Anya remembered the picture she had found in her dad's overall pocket. She didn't tell her brother about it, but just thought she would throw it in the pile with all the others once he brings them round.

He arrives around seven. and they have a coffee and some biscuits. Talin has also brought some of Dad's records with him.

"I thought you should have the Motown stuff and the soppy ones."

Anya smiles a thank you, and Talin puts them on her bookcase.

"Where shall we start?"

"Let's have a look first," says Talin, and promptly tips the first box upside down onto the living room floor, emptying the whole thing.

The two of them sit on the floor sifting through all the different images of holidays, family life, people they've never seen before, terrible out-of-focus ones, heads-cut-off ones, ones that are too dark and ones that are too bright.

"Jesus, didn't they have a decent phone back then?"

"Loads of these are from the seventies and eighties, idiot."

"Oh yeah. Still, the old cameras must have had a focus button or something?"

"Here's Mum and Dad stood next to the Mondeo. They must have just got it."

Talin hands Anya a small black-and-white photograph.

"Who's that?"

"That's grandma."

"Eh?"

"When she was young, probably around my age twenty-something."

"She was a model, was Nana. How come you didn't get any of them good looks, Sis?"

"Idiot."

The two of them are enjoying reminiscing. They look through the hundreds of photographs for hours. By the time they are on the third box, Anya has already ordered a pizza for the two of them. It has been delivered and they are tucking into it.

After several moments of chuckling at Talin's naked baby pictures, Anya sees a photograph that catches her eye. She studies it closer. It is her mum and someone who can only be that Laura. They are both young. They are smiling and laughing like the best of friends. They are seated on a bench on the seafront somewhere, eating ice cream, wearing sunglasses and seemingly having a whale of a time. It's difficult to see with the sunglasses on, but Anya thinks it is the same woman.

"That Mum on holiday?"

"Yes."

"Who's the other girl?"

"I don't know."

Anya turns the photograph over, but there is nothing written on it. She looks back at the image as Talin continues perusing through the box. The bench is outside a shopfront window. In the window is a reflection of the person taking the photograph. It's Dad.

While Talin eats the last slice of ham and mushroom pizza, Anya gets up and goes over to the bookcase. She opens a drawer and pulls out the other photograph of the mysterious Laura. She compares the two. Anya is sure it is her now. The same curly hair, the same long legs. Once again, she looks at the writing on the back.

*From your ever loving girl, Laura xx*

Anya sits back with her brother.

"What's that one?"

She passes it to him.

"Oh yeah, I think she was at Dad's funeral."

"What?"

"Yeah. Same curly hair, dead tall, proper old, though."

"I don't remember that. Are you sure?"

"Yeah, pretty sure."

"I don't remember her being there."

"You were pretty messed-up to be fair, sis, crying and that."

"And you're sure it was her?"

"She came up to me as we were leaving. I hung back to

talk to Uncle Remmy when you had got in the car. It was weird. She grabbed my hand and stared at me, said 'you look just like your dad,' then left."

"Why didn't you tell me this before?"

"Why would I? I asked Uncle Remmy who she was, and he had no idea, either." Talin looked at his sister's face. "What is it? ...Sis? ...Sis?"

Anya stops staring at the photograph and snaps out of her daze.

"Sorry, you want another brew?"

"Yes, please."

The two of them share out the photographs, with Talin taking most of the ones that had himself in them, and Anya taking all the old photographs of relatives he didn't know.

When they finish, she kisses him goodbye, and he goes home to the flat he shares with his two mates, Cliff and Moaty. She locks up and gets ready for bed. She takes the box of photographs that are now hers and puts it at the foot of her wardrobe. There is no need to talk to Talin about Laura, Anya has decided, but she might give Auntie Gita a call tomorrow to see if she knows who Laura is.

Of course, with one thing and another, Anya never does get around to calling Auntie Gita and she never mentions, or for that matter, remembers Laura again.

# BLACKBIRD

That was the thing about these 600mm lenses; you could see the skin blemishes on people's faces half a mile away. Sadie wiped the lens clean. She attached the telephoto to the camera body and clipped the plate onto the tripod. It was cold on top of the Co-op building, and she was glad she had brought a flask of tea and worn an extra layer. She checked her weather app to see if the forecast had changed. Still no rain. She put her phone away after double-checking it was on silent, then settled down on her plump green cushion.

Sadie scanned the trees around the apartment block opposite with her naked eyes, before something caught her attention. She trained the camera in the direction of the movement and focused in. House sparrows darting in and out of the bushes, chasing one another. Sadie looked at her notes and reminded herself of what she wanted to photograph. She put the blue notebook away and zoomed in on the outer branches of a large oak that was just in front of a third-floor window. A woman was doing yoga in her living room. Sadie pulled focus to the tips of the tree. More movement. A goldfinch. Its bright red face and yellow-black striped wings shimmered in the green leaves. It tilted its head as if looking at the woman through the glass, watching her stretch her limbs, seemingly interested. The woman wore bright red and yellow Lycra. Perhaps the bird thought she was one of them? Something else soon caught its attention and off it went.

Sadie had always thought that the birds watched us, just as much as we studied them. She remembered as a little girl going to her grandma's cottage in Devon and a robin would sit on the window-sill looking in on them. It seemed to seven-year-old Sadie that it would come at different times of the day, checking up on them, making sure they were okay. Hilda, which is what she named the bird, sat on the windowsill staring in watching them eat breakfast, looking at what was on the television, and seeing what book Sadie was colouring in that day. It was a sad day when Grandma's cat Oscar came sloping in one wet Sunday afternoon with Hilda in its mouth. The cat proudly dropped the dead bird at the foot of Gran's armchair and went back outside. Grandma had tried to tell Sadie it was not Hilda, but another robin. Sadie was unsure, but soon knew that her grandma was just trying to reassure her when there was no little scarlet-breasted face at the window anymore.

Stupid cat, thought Sadie.

A wood pigeon's melancholic cry came from nearby and brought Sadie out of her daydream. Sadie liked wood pigeons. Few people she knew did. They were silly, cumbersome, and not the brightest of our winged friends. But there was something gentle and lonely about them, too. And that call was so sad. She always felt they were a little depressed and needed a friend. How could you dislike something so forlorn? She looked around but couldn't see one. The sound had stopped.

She tilted the lens upward along the trunk of the tree until she reached the top and then glided out along the branch of the oak until she came to the end. This was right next to the window of a fifth floor flat. Nice large flat-screen TV, huge sound bar, no carpet, very little furniture, and a film poster framed on the back wall behind the black leather sofa. A young man entered the room, from what was probably the bedroom door. He was wearing a robe and looked like he had just gotten out of bed. The man made his way over to the kitchenette and prepared some filter coffee. He picked up a nearby remote and pointed it at nothing in particular. He paused what he was doing for a moment, stared at the wall, then nodded his head before proceeding with his breakfast preparations. Sadie couldn't hear the music, but assumed it was something awful.

More movement in the corner of her eye. She whip-panned across and glimpsed a magpie bouncing from branch to branch. Not a big fan of the magpie. Sadie always felt there was something wicked about them. She wasn't sentimental about birds. Predators had to eat and feed their own. She wasn't squeamish. Her opinion of the pied crow was because of its intelligence and sneakiness, that plus the day she saw three of them hunt down a rabbit kit on a grassy knoll, chasing and pecking it, seemingly prolonging the agony of the baby animal. They were like those three veloci-raptors from Jurassic Park, or a pod of orca tiring a seal. Working together, enjoying the hunt and terrifying the prey, more than just a primal need to kill for food. The cackle didn't help, either. An evil laugh.

Sadie checked her watch. 8:30am. This was the exact time that the target was supposed to get up. She looked at the apartment building opposite and counted four floors up, three windows in from the right. She trained the camera lens at that point, then panned from one side of the large window to the other. A living room similar to all the others, same shape, same size, but the décor in this one was littered with knick-knacks. An African tribal mask here, a ceramic elephant lamp there. All kinds of tacky souvenirs. Junk bought from airports from around the globe by a person who had no interest in where they were visiting, but wanted to show people they'd been there.

Movement. A corpulent, sixty-two-year-old man in a silk kimono walked over to the window and stared out at the street below. Sadie pressed the shutter and six or seven images of the man's face were recorded on the memory card. He opened the window and placed his left hand in his pocket, removing a folded piece of paper. He held his hands against the frame of the window as if leaning on it. If you had blinked, you would have missed the folded bundle falling from his hand into the street below, before he closed the window again and walked to his bathroom.

Sadie tried to get to where it had fallen. She eventually reached street level, but saw another man in a black suit pick up the paper and keep walking. He had his back to her, already on his way. She took a few shots anyway, knowing they were useless without his face. Sadie hadn't even get a shot of the action, but she knew he had scooped it up. She followed him as he strode down the street, farther out of reach. Then, just for a moment, she got lucky. He turned to look back to see if traffic was coming, before crossing the street. Still with him in focus, she held the shutter down. He was pretty far away, but she knew she could get something, maybe even enough of a clear image to identify him.

She whipped her attention back to the fat man's window.

The bathroom door was still closed. She took out her notebook and wrote down the times:

*8:30 appears at window*

*8:32 drops note*

*8:35 photo of contact*

She looked at her watch again, then put the notebook away.

9:37am. Over an hour in the bathroom. Sadie shivered at the thought of what he might have been up to behind the closed door for so long. He was now dressed, at least, in a white collared shirt and brown cotton trousers. He was still in his stockinged feet and padded across to the living area and sat down. Surprisingly, no breakfast for this big chap. He picked up a mobile phone that was charging on a coffee table, dialed, waited a moment, then started to talk.

Sadie took a frame. He laughed at something. His own joke, thought Sadie. He made a sweeping gesture with his left hand, which Sadie took to be his description of a smooth job done. Another small chuckle, a goodbye, and he rang off. He sat there for a moment, then smiled. Another shot.

The man whipped his head round, looking at the front door. A caller. He shuffled his frame to the end of the sofa and winched himself up onto his feet. The man trundled over to the door with Sadie's lens following him the entire way. He opened the door. No one came in, but he didn't leave. There was someone there, and he seemed to talk to them because she could see him gesturing with his hands. It was the same gesture used by an Italian footballer who had just committed a foul, and knew it, but was pleading to the referee for forgiveness. Then the back of his head exploded. His flaccid frame slumped to the floor. Another frame of him on the carpet with a hole in his forehead. Sadie panned up to the doorway. The door to his apartment was still wide open, but no one was there. She trained her lens on the shared front door of the apartment building and waited. Waited.

Must have gone out another way, she decided. She looked up at the window. Some people had gathered in the doorway of the fat man's apartment. One was on the phone. Another frame. Sadie picked up the notebook and wrote:

*10:01am shot through head*

*10:08am people gather*

She cleaned the lens before replacing the cap. Sadie removed the lens and put away the camera and tripod. She tidied away her notebook, pen, cushion, and flask. She gathered her equipment and made her way towards the fire escape back down to street level.

She could hear an ambulance siren getting closer as she exited the Co-op building on the same side as the apartment building across the way. She walked around the back of the Co-op building and put her stuff in the back of her car, locked it, then went back round the front. The ambulance and a police car had already arrived. She crossed the road towards where a uniformed officer stood.

The policeman stepped towards her. "Hang on, love. Do you live here?"

"No, I was just going to visit my friend."

"Which apartment?"

"It's Mary on the third floor. I don't know the number. We are going for a walk after she's done her exercises."

The young policeman looked unsure.

"I'll call her, so she knows I'm on my way up and just go straight there."

He looked her in the eyes, and Sadie gave nothing away.

"Go on then."

He stepped aside, and Sadie took out her phone and started a conversation as she walked towards the entrance. Once out of earshot, she abruptly stopped, but kept her phone in her hand. She went to the lift and pressed four.

No officers down here, she thought. There aren't enough of them here yet.

The elevator took her to the fourth floor, and the doors pinged open. She stepped out and looked down the hall to her left. A group of people had gathered around the entrance to the fat man's apartment. She casually walked to them. She kept walking past and squeezed beyond them, with no one taking much notice. They were all too busy looking inside. She went to the end of the corridor to the fire escape. She took one last look back down the corridor and opened the door. No alarm. She stepped inside to find concrete stairs, and descended.

Sadie reached the ground floor and looked out the door, but quickly shut it again. More police had arrived and were stationed in the lobby. It was the same entrance she had entered, and the one the killer did not leave by. She continued down the stairs, down another floor to a basement. She opened the door more carefully this time. No one about. It was a delivery area. There was an entrance for vehicles on the far side. She made her way in that direction. By the exit was a large plastic waste bin. She lifted the lid. A rancid stench filled her nostrils, and she recoiled. She took a deep breath and then looked inside. Atop the bags of rubbish was a trench coat. She reached inside and lifted it out by finger and thumb. Its bland beige sleeve was splattered with crimson. She dropped it back in and shut the lid down, as she had found it.

Sadie walked into the parking area behind the apartments and found several executive vehicles in numbered bays and a secure gate around ten-foot high. She made her way to a securely-locked double gate. On the street side was a camera and key code pad. She looked back at the building and around the perimeter.

Only one way in and out, she thought. She took a picture of the locked gate with her phone, then turned and took another of the entrance to the building. She looked up at the fourth floor and then about her to see if there were any other security cameras. None. Sadie chewed her thumbnail as she sometimes did when thinking. A nice block like this would have cameras everywhere, unless the occupants didn't want them.

As she stood there, a blackbird hopped out of a bush right next to her. It eyed her up and down, then scurried over to a worm that was slithering on the concrete. The bird scooped it up in its beak, looked back over at Sadie, then flew up onto the fence. It gulped down its meal, shook its feathers, then seemed to hear something which caught its attention. Then Sadie heard it too, another blackbird. When the other bird had finished, the one on the fence began its song. Sadie stood and listened.

A lovely varied tune from the blackbird, thought Sadie. It continued to sing and then halted, turned its head in the direction of the gate behind Sadie, and took flight.

The gates opened and a large silver four-by-four cruised in. Sadie stepped to one side and made sure her back was to the vehicle as it passed. She made her way out through the open gate and onto the street. The gates closed behind her. She did not look back to see who got out of the car.

# SAW

Howard is cutting logs on a bandsaw. He is quickly and expertly slicing down the wood. The farm has been a family residence and business for generations. Howard is the latest in a long line of Bentleys who have worked this land. The timber is taken from his own woodland, grown by his great-grandfather. Good, versatile pine. This will be used for firing the furnace and building the chicken coop that he needs to get done before the spring is out. He is glad he moved the machine nearer to the barn door last autumn, as today is warm and humid. The sun is on his back as the door is wide open, letting in what little breeze there is. As another piece hits the pile, he wipes his brow. He switches off the machine. He turns to pick up a flask and guzzles the contents in one until the vessel is empty. Now that he has stopped working, he can see a figure walking in the direction of the barn. He is a good distance away, but he strides purposefully, showing his intentions. Despite the yards and the sweat in his eyes, Howard recognises the waving man. Howard sighs and turns his back on the man and goes back to the saw.

Jeff finally arrives at the barn, assuming Howard didn't see or hear him coming. He catches his breath after walking up the long slope to the farm. Howard knows Jeff is standing behind him but carries on working.

"Howard...*Howard!*"

Howard turns but leaves the machine running. Still not speaking, forcing Jeff to continue awkwardly.

"Alice has signed."

"Good for her."

"Come on, Howard, just think what you could do with—"

"Save your breath."

Howard turns and switches off the saw. He picks up a handful of the cut wood and goes to pile it up at the back of the barn. Jeff watches him as he comes back for another load.

"It's a lot of money, Howard. The water company has got everyone on board except you. Even Alice. She needs the money, Howard. We all do."

Howard continues to ignore Jeff's pleas.

"Have you even looked at the prospectus?"

Howard pauses momentarily, then throws down the wood and walks over to Jeff, who instinctively takes a step backward. As he reaches where he is standing, he leans into Jeff and talks calmly and deeply into his ear.

"Listen, I don't know what you've said to Alice, but you better get off my land before I do something both of us might regret."

As he finishes, he stares into Jeff's eyes. He is at least a foot taller and much broader than Jeff, who lowers his eyes. Howard walks out of the barn towards the farm. He is finished talking.

As he disappears out of view, Jeff stands there. He stares

at the open door towards the way he arrived. He takes one step forward, then stops, looking back at the band saw, then again at the barn door. Jeff kneels down in front of the saw, looking underneath for something. He seems to find what he is looking for and reaches in. He unscrews a bolt and puts it in his pocket. He leaves the same way he came, but this time with a little more haste.

# CAMINO DIARIES

Dear Mrs Baikie,

I was pleased we got to speak on the phone the other day. It has been so long since we last spoke and I am not surprised that you had all but given up hope of ever finding your son Samuel and his friend Jayne. The recent events that have transpired were a big surprise to us and to the authorities here in the UK. We have requested that the Spanish police send back the ruck sack and belongings that were discovered, but we are unsure how long this will take. A representative from the British embassy has been able to obtain a copy of your son's diary, which was in the rucksack, and we are sending this to you via a courier in the morning. Although we hope the Spanish authorities will re-open the case, there is very little we can do from here at this present time. We have arranged for the diary to be translated into Spanish and sent back in the hope it may prompt them into finding some clue as to Samuel's disappearance, and we hope you find some solace in your son's words. We will speak soon.

**William Morris CLSA**

*Morris and Micklewhite Solicitors*

~

**15th July 1997**

*Roncesvalles*: Day one—or is it day two? We've now spent forty-eight hours on a bus. After only realising we travel on a coach rather than ferry, whilst in mid-journey, we've also decided that we seem to be making this up as we go along. So far, we have not been able to wash, clean our teeth or sleep for these whole two days, and even caused physical harm to one another (by accident). We have so far managed to stay friends.

Not being used to "roughing" it, I found myself at a point where I noticed I was frowning rather heavily. Even though I had realised my social faux pas, I found that I could do nothing about it—I simply couldn't smile. That was until we reached the final part of the never-ending bus ride. We travelled up and up into the mountains. It seemed like we were never going to come down again.

After very little sleep the past two days, I was barely with it, until I looked out of the window. Even a cynic like me couldn't fail to be impressed with the view. Then, I looked to my side and could swear I saw a similar expression on the face of my friend. I think at this point our torture had ended, and our journey had begun. All we had to do now was to check in, wash up and prepare ourselves for whatever lay ahead.

**16th July 1997**

*Zubiri*: Today has, like the hills we've walked through, had its ups and downs. We've achieved more than we thought we would have—twenty-four kilometres. But at a price. My friend's feet have blistered badly, and my old football injury (a dodgy knee ligament) is hurting like mad. This is because of the bad terrain we have had to travel across. It's so bad you have to judge almost every step you take. This we got used to and managed quite healthily with plenty of provisions and friendly hellos along the way.

About ten kilometres away from Zubiri (our destination of rest), a thunderstorm and torrential rain fell on us from nowhere. We had no waterproofs, and we were drenched instantly. This was okay as long as it was still warm and we were still walking, but once we reached Zubiri we stopped and felt cold and tired. So, we headed for the hostel. At this point, all I wanted was a hot shower and a hot meal. When we reached the hostel, there was no room at the inn. So much for the certain places to stay from the nice Christian folk.

Faced with walking another twelve kilometres to the next town and being drenched and tired wasn't really an option. So with the help of three Spanish women, we went to a local bar which pointed us in the direction of a hotel. At around £35 for the night for a double en-suite room, this was going to eat into our budget—but desperation had already gripped. As I'm writing this, neither of us has had a hot meal because the hotel has nothing and we cannot afford to wet any more clothes by going outside. Our rations are low; our morale is lower. Talk of quitting is imminent. If we don't manage to get waterproofs, petrol for the stove and more food and water—if we manage to get out without another storm—then I honestly don't know what we'll do.

### 17th July 1997

*Trinidad de Arre*: What a difference a day makes. It's just after 3pm, and we've not only arrived in time but showered, changed, hung out our wet clothes, filled the stove up with fuel, bought fresh bread and eaten a hot meal and drunk a hot drink. We have a bed to sleep on, and we've seen some familiar friendly faces. Our morale is now much higher although I've now got my first blister, and it's a big one. My knee is still painful. I'm a little worried this will slow us down and possibly cause permanent damage.

We're now resting before going out later this afternoon to get some more provisions. The walk was okay, apart from the three inches of mud on a single track on a mountainside. A little precarious at times, but our luck held out and we arrived here. I like the mornings best. Quiet and peaceful, and we rarely see others, just stunning countryside, postcard villages and each other's company.

These old hostels seem so sad. The simplicity of it, the religious artefacts and pictures littered all around them. There is a painting of Mary holding (what looks like a miniature adult Jesus) the baby Jesus. It's flaky, it has no frame, but it looks quite beautiful. Maybe it isn't Mary and child, perhaps the child is a depiction of the travellers being looked after by the mother of all mothers herself.

Am I finally getting some sort of religion? I doubt it, well nothing so spiritual. Although I never thought that I would appreciate a hot bowl of soup and bread as much as I did this afternoon. Maybe now or perhaps much later, I will actually be less depressed about trivial things and will learn to re- evaluate my values. It's a little bit early to predict life changes, but I think we may have overcome our fears and started to appreciate things.

Met a man in his forties at the entrance to the hostel. He seemed reluctant to talk. Couldn't place the accent—Eastern European? Not as friendly as most we've met. Friend thought he was Bosnian.

**18th July 1997**

*Cizur Menor*: Last night was special. One table, one meal, one bottle of wine and five nationalities. We talked for hours about many things, mainly Ricardo, the Indian boy from Brazil and his journey to see his people deep in the rainforest of his home country. Through Anna, a Swiss woman who spoke German, English and Spanish, the whole table could communicate. The others being myself, friend, Christian a nineteen-year-old from Germany and Carl from Israel.

We broke bread, we drank red wine from a local vineyard and we spoke at length about Ricardo's spiritual journey, and through Anna, he told us the whole story. Not just his journey, but his life, his people, the sacred stone he always carried around his neck. We asked questions, and he seemed flattered that we were interested. Well, friend and I were. Christian was more interested in the mind-altering drugs that the tribe prepared and gave to Ricardo and Carl. Well, Carl was like he always was, half asleep. This is one of the things I imagined this camino to be like: friendly, welcoming and interesting. All except the Bosnian (as we now call him). We invited him to the dinner, but he declined and sat outside the window smoking cigarettes.

The hostels so far have gotten better, from sleeping on the floor at Roncesvalles to a hot shower and a bed in Zubiri, and now a bunk bed, hot shower, hot meal and glorious garden to sit and write this down in the afternoon sun. If the rest of the refugios (pilgrim hostels) are like this one all the way along, I'll be more than happy. Our feet hurt. Friend's are especially bad. She has at least six blisters, and at one point, I didn't think that she was going to make it this far. We saw the cathedral in Pamplona, we bought postcards, and finally we had waterproofs. Of course, as soon as we bought these, the sun decided to shine. The lady of the house appears to be a writer. She seems to live on her own in a huge house and runs this scenic, clean and friendly hostel. It looks like something out of a novel, maybe one of her novels. All I know is it's a calm, peaceful and homely place. This could be a good holiday, if only our feet let it happen.

### 19th July 1997

*Puenta la Reina*: Today, we walked nineteen kilometres. And (touch wood) it may be a little easier. On our walk, the Bosnian passed us. We saluted him with the usual pilgrim greeting, but he ignored us. He is either very unfriendly, or perhaps his English is not so good. We arrived in Puenta la Reina at 2pm, stamped our passports and booked into our beds. I'm not so keen on the refugio. It reminds me of a prisoner of war camp. Four rows of three high bunk beds all lined up with little room to move. (I doubt I'll get much sleep tonight. In Spain, there seems to be a snorer every other person.) Without thinking, I shared my thoughts on prisoner of war camps with Christian, who seemed a little bemused, especially when halfway through I realised what I was saying and who to, and dug myself in deeper and deeper.

I seem to have the strangest sunburn ever. On the back of my calf is a six-inch square that is red, apart from a small strip where a plaster was. It looks very silly and is very sore. Friend seems to have a similar strip that goes from her forehead, over her ear and on to her neck. How did we miss these bits with the suncream?

We met Ricardo again today. We sat outside eating French bread and cream cheese. With our phrase books, he learnt English and us Spanish and Portuguese. He wants us to meet up again tomorrow in Estella, our next port of call for lesson two. Asked him what he thought of the Bosnian, and he didn't seem to know who we meant. We also met our first English person today. A young lad from Devon travelling with a Swiss boy, a French boy and a lad from Honduras. I'm quite surprised at so many peregrinos (pilgrims) not speaking Spanish. Our Spanish is crap, but compared to some, we're natives. Each day has been different from the last, so I wonder what tomorrow holds.

### 20th July 1997

*Estella*: It's the end of the week, and a whole week of walking has taken its toll. It took us nearly eight hours to walk to Estella today. It's twenty kilometres again, but today was hot. The route was unshaded practically the whole way, and the sun beating down on us slowed our pace, sapped our energy and drained our morale. The fact that this was the third day running I've had no sleep probably adds extra weight to an already heavy burden. At one point, not far from Estella, I thought that I wasn't going to make it. We thought that the town was just around the corner, and when we went round the corner, it wasn't there, so we sat a while, drank lots of water and tried to muster up not only some strength but more importantly some willpower to go on. Obviously, we knew we had to. We were in the middle of nowhere with only provisions for one day. Eventually, we dragged ourselves to our feet, pulled on our hair shirts (our rucksacks) and soldiered on. The hostel was clean, comfortable and had lots of amenities (including a wonderful power shower, which was just what we needed) and was a real sight for sore feet. Tomorrow, we decided, will be our rest day. We shall get the bus to Los Arcos and rest at the refugio there. And hopefully some sleep, too.

### 21st July 1997

*Los Arcos*: Today was our day of rest. Last night, I managed a few hours of sleep, and today we took the bus (twenty kilometres) to Los Arcos. Guess who was on the bus? That's right the Bosnian. I tried to make eye contact as we walked past down the aisle, but he looked away and pretended not to notice us. He sat at the back on his own, not speaking to anyone.

The weather is getting hotter, my knee still hurts and I've left my stick at the last refugio, so tomorrow is going to be bad. It's around seventeen kilometres to Logrono, which is the longest part of our trip, so I hope to get plenty of rest and, most importantly, sleep for tomorrow.

Our so-called day of rest has allowed us to get things done. We've changed traveller's cheques at the bank, bought more food and water, attempted to buy something light for our feet (but for some reason all the shoe shops were shut) and more film for the camera.

The refugio is nice and clean. With us getting here nice and early, we managed to do our washing and hang it out in the midday sun to get dry. The place seems to be run by a Belgian couple who speak good English and have signs up around the place in many languages. I've actually tried using more Spanish today, ordering the bus tickets, finding the times and the place of the bus, buying the food and film etc. It isn't ideal, but I've found if I adopt a Spanish accent, I seem to be better understood. Maybe that's nonsense, but it seems to be so.

We've met our first friendly locals. A nice man in a little shop and an understanding lady in a pharmacy. I think Ricardo is after his second English lesson. We've been pulling Carl's leg (maybe that's why it hurts so much?) about him travelling on the bus for the whole camino. We had one day of rest. He seems to have had one day walking. Some of the cyclists are going to the swimming pool down the road and asked if we wanted to go. Unfortunately, with friend's feet just starting to heal it's probably a bad idea. But in this heat, it sounds so inviting. Maybe we'll get another opportunity further down the line. Carl has decided to go for a ride. When friend asked him if he rides well, he replied "I don't know I find out today." It's good to know how many other people have no idea what they're doing, too. Knowledge is fear; ignorance is bliss.

We took a walk around the town and had some ice cream. Friend commented on how strange it must be to live in one of these small villages. There seems to be lots of bars but little life. The towns are full of older people, but very few young people. Maybe they've moved to the city or perhaps there's a certain time when the young people come out. In Estella last night, there was some kind of medieval market. That was bustling with lots of young people. But that's the first and only time we've seen them en masse. Could have sworn I saw the Bosnian. He seemed to be following us. Probably not.

### 22nd July 1997

*Viana*: It's been an indifferent day. The refugio is a scruffy, not well maintained, cold place. It's been pouring with rain for most of the day and my knee is causing me great pain. Usually, it's difficult to walk at the end of the day with it stiffening up and aching. Today around eight kilometres along from our destination (Viana) I twisted it and could hardly walk. It's a pity because we would have made it in excellent time after our rest day and the cooler weather. In fact, the first ten kilometres we passed walkers who left an hour before us. We weren't running. We simply walked through the downpour, whereas everyone else seemed to hide from the rain. I guess living in the North of England has hardened us to the more extreme elements (except sun and heat). The rain was so hard, rivers flowed through the streets of the villages. Small children could easily have been swept away. Our arrival in Viana has been like that of most of our destinations; greeted with inner elation and a sense of relief. We are lucky to arrive just as the town was preparing itself for its own festival. Everyone was in the streets. Music was playing and the men were building an arena for the grand finale of the day—the bull run. We'd heard that it was at 2pm. So after dropping off our things at the refugio and changing, we headed back to the bustling centre. Christian had decided to run with the local boys and tied his hair in to two bunches like horns (much to the local people's amusement). Friend got a good view, hanging on to the fence right next to where the bulls went by, to take photographs. When it started the people cheered and whistled and the men and boys started to run and jump on to the barriers while five small, frightened and confused bullocks were harassed and prodded four or five times along the Calle Mayor. We took a couple of photographs and laughed at young Christian and were quickly underwhelmed and then just felt sorry for the poor animals. The Bosnian showed his face. This time we got a nod of recognition. Progress at last. Maybe he is a lost soul? Who knows why people do this pilgrimage? Especially the loners like the Bosnian. As for Christian, I think he impressed the two young Spanish girls that he's been trying to chat up ever since Puenta la Reina. We've managed an hour siesta and may even limp out to check out the evening's festival activities. Apparently, there's music in the streets, through the night—I doubt we'll be dancing.

**23rd July 1997**

*Logrono*: A nice steady eight kilometres today. It took us only two hours. We arrived in Logrono at 10.30am, but the refugio didn't open until 3pm. Fortunately, the cleaning women let us put our rucksacks inside, and we wandered the town. Last night was comforting. The refugio was awful, and the noisy people were right next door to us. The men's toilet was overflowing with piss, and the shower was covered in mildew, but we had a whole room to ourselves in the end. James, the young English boy, went next door, so friend and I slept in the same bunk. It was nice. Friend went straight to sleep. We were both awoken in the middle of the night by Christian. Friend thought she had dreamt it at first, but can two people have the same dream? Around 2am, the door to the room swung open, and there he stood, swaying from too much beer, his hair in two spikes, silhouetted by the moonlight. He paused for a moment, scanned the room and shouted to the room next door, "Are they dead?" then shut the door again.

It was a rapturous day for our feet. We finally found some cheap, lightweight footwear. A perfect breather to wear when we are not walking. And just for three hundred pesetas each. We also explored the small city and went inside the cathedral. It seemed strange to me that tourists and locals still use it for prayer, and confession and were mixing together. I felt like an intruder really. There were no signs up saying don't take pictures, but it seemed inappropriate. It was quite a grand place. Although it was dark and hardly lit, you could still see all the wealth emblazoned around in the glory of God. I always have a problem with that. It just seems to me that it's the prayer not the statue that matters, the faith not the silk and the gold robes. Surely, all that money could be put to better use? Another strange phenomenon I've noticed while here, is the churches close up shop and only open for mass. Aren't these places supposed to be sanctuaries, especially for the pilgrim. I guess that's why we have the refugio in modern times. The church has no time for charity. I wonder if the local padres know the story of the Good Samaritan. But then, who's an agnostic like me to criticise the church and interpret the Bible? Charity begins at home, and the home of God is closed for lunch. As we sit in the pews, a sensation of being watched comes over me. I look around to see a familiar face, the Bosnian. A smile and a nod; progress indeed. I guess he approves of our visit.

Tomorrow will be tough. Twenty-six kilometres. We've never attempted anything of this length since the first day (twenty-four kilometres). But then we had fresh feet and legs. Now friend's feet look like bubble wrap. Her ankles have swollen as if she were pregnant and with my knee—if I was a horse, I'd have been shot!

We have walked an average four kilometres an hour, so with breaks we estimate our arrival at Najera at 2pm. There's only one stop in between at Naverette (ten kilometres in to the journey) which has no refugio so it's a one-way trip and no other way out. I just hope we make it. We have to. It would be a crap way to die. It would be ironic if I did, though. When stories come on the news about some English person stranded on a mountain in Tibet or a yachtsman drowned off the Philippines, I'm always the first to say, "Well, that's their own fault. They knew what they were doing. Why didn't they get a real job and stop pissing about?" Alas, fate may laugh at the cold-hearted.

Tonight was another language lesson with Ricardo. His English is a one hundred times better than my Spanish. If we were in the same school, I'd be held back a year. He also taught, or rather showed, us how the Indians do their calls.

Neither myself nor friend could do it. Ricardo said that it took him a week. We also talked about his homeland, where his parents live in Brazil, "the mountains, the rivers, the trees" as he put it. High above us, as we sat on the patio of the refugio, storks stand balanced on one leg on the stonework of the monastery. As they clatter their beaks, we learn how Germany and Israel also tell of the bird that carries the babies. The bird had so many names, too. In English it is one thing, Spanish another, Portuguese, Hebrew, German, etc. Yet the mosquito, it seems, is always the mosquito. Maybe it's harder to describe more beautiful, graceful things than it is to describe the things that we dislike and find unappealing. I ask Carl about the Bosnian. He didn't seem to know who we were talking about, either.

**24th July 1997**
*Najera*: No Entry.

**25th July 1997**
*Azofra*: All I can say about yesterday is that I'm glad it's all over. Today, we walked just six kilometres to Azofra. It's a rest day. The rest of the pilgrims we've met have gone on to the next town, but our bodies can't go where we want them to go. My knee still aches and lack of sleep leaves me jaded. As for friend, her feet are so bad she can't stand, let alone trek for long distances. She was close to tears yesterday. Needless to say, our morale is very, very low. As for Azofra, well, it looks like we will be spending the feast of St. James here.

All the locals seem to be milling about town, anxious, waiting for something. As for us, we seem to be the only two pilgrims here. Even though we want to do this on our own, and we walk alone and spend our evenings alone, it's always nice to see a friendly, familiar face at the refugio. We feel lost.

It's really frustrating that our bodies won't do what we want them to do. We're not going to push ourselves as hard anymore. Fifteen kilometres a day is enough, no more twenty-six kilometres days in the scorching heat. And when there are gaps of thirty kilometres (there's a forty-one kilometres in one place) then the bus is our only safe option. I don't think of it as cheating, just living. Something is definitely happening in Azofra. Cars with loudspeakers keep driving past. The past couple of day's events made us recognise our limits. We'll get to Santiago somehow, even if we walk five kilometres and bus thirty kilometres. I'd rather enjoy it and be awake and healthy enough to see all these glorious sights and wonderful things—not just walk, bleed and sleep.

The elderly couple who run this refugio are really nice. Neither speaks a word of English, but their friendliness is universal. Despite the welcome the small refugio offers, and the fact that we have had three hours sleep this afternoon (which was more than needed) we feel low today. Maybe it's because we've got no goal, no mission to walk so many kilometres, to find the refugio, to stock up on provisions and to try and catch some sights.

After our siesta, we seem at a loss for something to do. We bought some things to eat and walked down to the Fountain of Romeros just on the edge of town. But our minds were wandering, and we sat in silence and stared in to space. Normally, we relax and enjoy our surroundings and contemplate everything and anything, together and with anyone who wishes to join in.

It's now a quarter to ten. We've eaten. (We finally mustered up the energy to cook something—omelettes.

That's English style omelettes, not tortilla española. A Spanish omelette is an egg and potato sandwich, which is fine, but I like the way that I cook them). Then we showered and climbed into bed.

A few peregrinos have arrived: a middle-aged French couple, the Bosnian, a young Spanish couple on bicycles, and I think the old German man on horseback had decided to stay here. The Spanish couple told us they heard of a pilgrim that had gone missing and has not been heard of since Logrono. Gustav, the older German man, said he had overhead a Swedish couple talking of a missing man but didn't know the details. When we went around the room, the rest of us stated we hadn't heard anything, and the Bosnian also shook his head, but then quickly left us. He is very unfriendly.

### 26th July 1997

*Santo Domingo de la Calzada*: It's all quiet now. We're in Santo Domingo de la Calzada, and the hostel is full of sleeping people. All these pilgrims are having a siesta. It makes a nice change. It's quiet now, but earlier a brass band was playing outside with people dancing and clapping. The mornings are always alive on Saturdays, but not as lively as the evenings.

Earlier when wandering through the town, we saw a strange busker. He looked like some post-apocalyptic minstrel, dressed in a combination of rags and period costume. He was on a bicycle clad in similar attire and playing a flute through an amplifier and banging his knees together for rhythm with cymbal and bells attached to them. This town seems quite a tourist trap, and they were lapping up his performance. They also seem to sell a lot of pilgrim and camino souvenirs. Who are they selling them to; the peregrinos or the tourists? Maybe both.

I think that we are going to cook up something tasty tonight and have a bottle of Rioja with it. It's an attempt to remember that we're actually on a break. It's been twelve days now, and I'm finally beginning to miss something—a cup of tea. How terribly English of me.

### 27th July 1997

*Belorado*: Well we're finally back in the saddle, so to speak. We managed twenty-one kilometres and arrived in Belorado (or Eldorado as friend called it) just after 2pm. Today is a scorcher. I'm not sure what the temperature is exactly, but it has to be in the nineties.

Unfortunately, because we arrived at 2pm, everywhere is shut and we can't eat anything substantial. The only places open are bars, but friend's confidence in the local cuisine is more than suspicious. We're now in our third Provence and have in total travelled 194 kilometres. We're a little behind schedule, but it's our rest day tomorrow, so we'll keep moving like we did before and travel to our next stop by bus. That's if we can find a bus stop in this place. It's not as bad as our guide book makes it sound. If we can't, then the prospect of walking twenty kilometers in the afternoon sun is not one that I relish. This place is tiny, very few people are here. In fact, we have only seen one old woman since arriving. The refugio looks shut. I hope it opens sometime soon.

Finally, I see another soul, the Bosnian. He sees us and comes over. Rather surprisingly, he starts a conversation. His English is very good. He asks us what are plans are and we ask him if this refugio is going to open. He seems to think it will and tells us to wait with him by the river. The guy seems like a different person, so friendly. Friend is not so sure. She says we will follow him down there, but he insists on us coming with him. He seems to be looking for someone as well, looking over our shoulders and all around him. I ask him if he is looking for someone and he says no, just us. I say I am just going to write today's entry in my diary. He looks agitated, but says he'll wait. Time to go down to the river.

Looking forward to tomorrow, over halfway there now.

# THE ORANGE QUESTION

The Saturday:

*One hour? That's nowhere near enough time. At the semi-finals, we had two hours and access to a library and the internet. Now, it is either go into the rec room or sit on a beanbag and we are not allowed a phone.* Terry looked around him. People were making notes, looking in the air, thinking, then making notes. Terry bit the skin around his thumbnails. He always chews dead skin flakes off his digits when he is anxious, but now he was gnawing down to the raw flesh. When he realised he was doing it, he instinctively looked behind him, expecting a cuff around the head from his Aunt Edith. But Aunt Edith had died last year. A strict woman, always angry at something. Usually Terry. No wonder her heart gave way at the age of sixty-two.

Terry sighed. He gathered himself and started to clear his mind. It was a meditation technique he had learnt from Simon the Guru, a new-age YouTuber that Terry followed. Breathe slowly and think of a beach, an empty beach. Water laps the shore. The sun is rising (or possibly setting, it didn't matter which) on the horizon. Breathe. You see footprints in the sand. Breathe. Follow the footprints. Breathe. They are your own footprints. Breathe slower. You feel the soft wet ground squelch between your toes as you place your foot inside the perfect fitting footprint.

"Can I take your contestant number, please?"

Terry opens his eyes to see a freckle-faced girl with a blue woolly hat on, holding a clipboard and pen and waiting.

"Can I take your contestant number, please?"

Terry holds up his lanyard. "TB1138."

"Lovely. Sorry for waking you up."

"I wasn't asleep. I was…"

But the girl had already moved on. He looked at his watch. Nine minutes gone already, only fifty-one left. He decided to shelve Simon the Guru's beach therapy and get scribbling. Opening the first page of the loose leaf lined A4 pad that all the finalists had been given, he took a biro out of his Captain Scarlet pencil case. He unconsciously put the tip of the biro in his teeth, then wrote the question at the top of the page. "What does orange mean to you?"

**Two weeks before the Saturday:**

"The runner-up of the Think of an Answer north-west regional semi-final is…" Nobody in the hall at Caldwell Leisure Centre held their breath. "…Terry Black!"

There was a smattering of polite applause as Terry went up onto the hastily made podium to receive a certificate and a handshake from the right honourable Doris Ramsbottom, Mayoress. She forced a grimace at him.

"Well done."

"Thanks."

"And the winner of the Think of an Answer north-west regional semi-final is...Cynthia Gibbons!" A woman in her sixties wearing a nylon dress and with suitably overly long arms skipped up to receive her prize. She got a certificate, a handshake and a twenty-pound book token.

Doris proudly adjusted the ostentatious gold chain around her neck before being prodded by Gavin, the adjudicator from Darius Global Research, the organisers of the competition. He reminded her of her announcement duties. "And of course Cynthia will go onto...what?" More ear whispering from Gavin. "Cynthia and Terry will go onto the national finals being held in Wolverhampton in two weeks' time."

The thirty or so people who were gathered around quickly dispersed, and the sports hall was soon empty, but for the two contestants and Gavin from Darius Global Research.

"Thanks for staying behind," slimed Gavin, before moving between Terry and Cynthia, placing an arm around each and gently ushering them along as he talked.

"We will, of course, arrange travel for the finals. You will both be picked up by taxi from your houses—I will arrange a time by text message closer to the day—and you will be taken to the Dover Discount Hotel which is just around the corner from the National Exhibition Centre, which is near to Worsley Public Hall where we will hold the finals."

"The same taxi?" asked Terry.

"No, no, Terry, you will have one each, no expense spared by DGR."

Cynthia looked relieved.

They reached the exit. Gavin gave them both a gentle push outside, took one step back inside the door and with a last goodbye, closed it. Terry and Cynthia looked awkwardly at each other, before Terry took the lead.

"I guess I will see you there?" Cynthia nodded.

"Well done." A brief smile. Terry was about to speak again, but Cynthia interjected.

"Bye then." She swiftly walked in the direction of the car park to an awaiting brown Austin Allegro. Terry watched her get in the passenger side and saw it chug away. He looked at his certificate. It read *Runner-Up Of The Think of an Answer North-west Regional Semi-Final* in a gold san-serif, while underneath written in green felt-tip was *Terry Block*.

"Typical."

He folded the certificate and put it in the pocket in the back of his jeans and walked home.

**The Thursday before the Saturday:**

Terry had been on the phone with Gavin from Darius Global Research for just two minutes to receive his instructions, which were then sent to him again via text message. He was to be picked up Friday afternoon at 3:30pm by Maxi-Taxis. It will be prepaid and a single non-smoking room at the Dover Discount Hotel will await him. It was a good job Gavin did ring, as Terry had almost forgotten about Saturday. He had been so busy at work, he had not had time to even think about not winning the semi-final and the actual final itself. So many people seemed to be trading in old DVDs at the film-exchange shop where he worked, he had been run off his feet and had slumped down in front of his television every evening after work and fallen asleep. He never did have much stamina.

He had gotten lucky with the semi-final. Lawrence at work had told him about the competition as his mum Doris the Mayoress was guest of honour. He also told him what the question for the competition would be as his mum had let it slip by mistake and told him not to mention it, but it would be okay to tell him as he would not tell anyone, but told Terry. Lawrence thought Terry should enter because he was the shop genius. Those were Lawrence's words, not Terry's. His status as shop genius was based on his vast knowledge of several 1980s sitcoms, and nothing else. And his only competition for this title was Lawrence and Doug, the owner.

The semi-final question was "What invention would you un-invent?" Terry had thought of his idea the night before and had done some research, even before being allowed two hours and access to the library next door to the leisure centre and free Wi-Fi on the day. A clap-o-meter decided the winners, measuring the enthusiasm of the contestants' answers from the live crowd. He knew this audience would be mostly Luddite pensioners and tailored his answer accordingly. He would "un-invent mobile phones". It had worked a treat. Well, almost. Cynthia answered with "foreign call centres". This seemed to have been even more popular with the boomer brigade.

Now Terry had no heads-up on the question. He had nothing to research. No idea who the audience would be in Wolverhampton. No clue what-so-ever. He was seriously thinking of pulling out. But the allure of an all-expenses paid weekend away was too much. There was a prize for the national winner as well. A monthly subscription to Crossword Puzzle Magazine, a Darius Global Research mouse mat, and a week's holiday in Wales for two, including meal vouchers at Pizza Express and free passes to a castle of your choice.

I won't win, but I may as well have a go, he thought. Terry turned on the TV and fell asleep. It had been another busy day at the film-exchange shop.

$$\sim$$

**The Friday before the Saturday:**

The journey in the Maxi-Taxi was fairly uneventful, except for a near miss on the M6 where Faisal, his driver, was so busy talking and turning around to face Terry that he veered into the inside lane and nearly drove into the back of a dough-boy bread delivery van.

"Hello, my name is Leslie. Welcome to the Dover Discount Hotel. Can I take you name please?"

"Black, Terry Black."

"Thank you, Mister Black. Yes, here you are. Oh...hang on." Leslie turned and shouted in the side door to an office.

"Mrs Brooking!" Leslie continued staring at Terry with a big smile on her face. A short, frumpy woman bounded out of the office with a boarding-school girl sporty gait.

"Mr Black, may I extend a hearty Dover welcome to you and hope you have a marvellous stay with us."

"Thanks," said an unenthused and rather taken aback Terry.

"I'll take care of Mister Black, Leslie."

"Yes, Mrs Brooking." Leslie seemed disappointed.

"Gavin from DGR has left you a surprise in your room, Mister Black."

There was a pause as Terry waited to hear what it was, but Mrs Brooking took off on a different road.

"Here is your room key. Number 237. All the Think of an Answer finalists are on the second floor. You are the first to arrive." She slapped the key down on the counter.

"Thanks, again." Terry picked up the key and made his way to the lift. He arrived at the correct floor and opened the door labelled 237 and went in. Bed, wardrobe, en suite, hairdryer, twelve inch TV and a trouser press, all present and correct. He closed the door and threw his bag on the bed. He went over to the desk where an envelope and a bottle of £5.99 sparkling white wine sat. Inside the envelope is a card with the GDR logo on, and a printed message:

*Congratulations, Think of an Answer Finalist! Welcome, have a drink on us. Please come down to the Pat Roach Memorial Room at 6:30pm for aperitifs, and mingle with your fellow contestants.*

*Yours,*

*Gavin Thurston, L.E.P.*

Terry had a shower and changed into a shirt with a collar. By the time he was ready, the bottle of sparkling wine was empty.

Terry entered the Pat Roach Memorial Room at the designated time, saw it was already pretty full, and went straight to the bar.

"What's the local bitter?"

"That would be Old Chuff or, if you like a pale ale, we have Shirley's Curlies?"

Terry looked at the bespoke pumps. The bitter had a

picture of a bird in a flat cap with a pipe and the other was a rather saucy buxom woman winking.

"I'll try the chuff, please."

The barman poured the draft beer, then Terry paid and had a sip, nearly spilling it down himself when he felt a sturdy slap on his shoulder.

"Terry! Welcome."

Terry turned to see the gurning face of Gavin Thurston, immaculately dressed as usual, in a three-piece pinstripe suit and tie.

"Gavin."

"Come meet some of the others."

The hand remained on the shoulder, then gripped harder and pulled him towards the centre of the room. Terry clung to his pint. They glided over towards four middle-aged women sat at a round table drinking cocktails.

"Ladies, this is Terry, north-west runner-up. Terry this is, from left to right, Maureen and Louise south-west finalists, Karen and Mishka from the East Coast."

"Hello," they all said in unison; then carried on the conversation they were having before Gavin interrupted them.

"And over here..." Once again, Terry was physically urged to proceed by the over-bearing Gavin, "...is Colin from the north-east and Sanjay who is a local boy, both runners-up like yourself, Terry."

Colin extended his hand and Terry shook it, followed by Sanjay.

"I'll leave you gents to get acquainted."

Gavin slithered off to annoy someone else.

"Pillock," muttered Sanjay.

"Where you from, Terry?" inquired Colin. A small and pleasantly faced bald man in his early fifties.

"Bolton originally."

Sanjay was still looking in Gavin's direction as he did his rounds.

"Does he make anyone else's skin crawl?"

"Sanjay is not a fan of Mister Thurston, you'll gather. Can't say I am either. He's a canny fella, though. Knows how to wind people up."

"Smarmy bastard," Sanjay snarled, bringing a brief chuckle from Colin. Terry also smiled, reassured that he was not the only one who didn't care for Gavin. "I'm getting another Coke. Can I get you fellas anything?"

"I'm good, thanks," said Terry as Colin shook his head. Sanjay went over to the bar to get himself a drink, constantly looking around to see where Gavin was so he didn't have to bump into him again.

"So who do you think's gonna win, lad?" asked Colin.

"Not me."

"Word on the street has it that Gareth Harper-Crouch is the one to watch. South-east winner." Colin leaned in conspiratorially and lowered his voice. "Tall, thin fella over by the fruit machine on his own. Blond hair, glasses, and nose the size of Concord."

Terry nodded and glanced over Colin's shoulder to see the exact match of his description. He was eating pork scratchings and licking his fingers after each one.

"Eww."

"He told Yuhang, the guy who came runner up to him, that he had an IQ of 225, and his uncle invented the big baby computer."

"You thought they would put some money behind the bar," griped Sanjay on his return.

"Just telling Terry here about the bookie's favourite, Sanjay."

"The nerd?" Sanjay looked at Terry. "You tried having a conversation with him yet?"

Terry shook his head.

"Well, let's just say there's a reason he is stood on his own."

Terry looked over at the Think of an Answer champion in waiting, who had finished the pork scratchings and was folding the bag into a neat little triangle. He put it in a nearby ashtray and turned his attention to the fruit machine. He was inspecting every inch of it and reading all the instructions and serial numbers, but did not seem to want to put any money into it.

"We're gonna go to Sanjay's room and watch Morse if you fancy it, Terry?"

"No thanks. I'm a bit knackered. I think I might just go to bed."

Sanjay looked at his watch. "It's seven o'clock."

"Been a busy week at work."

"Well, we'll see you tomorrow, lad. Good luck," said Colin.

"You too, you two."

**The Saturday:**

Terry looked up at the large analogue clock ticking away in the public hall. Just under forty minutes left and still nothing. Not one idea. He looked around the room at all the other finalists. All seem to be casually scribbling away in their pads. He looked from person to person until he reached Maureen from the south-west, who stared right back at him disapprovingly. He quickly looked down at his pad. When he felt the coast was clear, he continued scanning the room.

At the back nearest the toilets was Gareth Harper-Crouch. He was furiously writing, fast and flowing, without pausing. Terry watched him as he intensely penned what could only be the winning answer. What the hell could he be writing about? thought Terry. Then, without warning, he slammed the pen down, shut the pad, folded his arms and shut his eyes. He sat still, not moving. Is he asleep? Exhausted by the intense work? Then, slowly, the corners of his mouth crept upward. Until finally a broad smile spread across his face.

*He's got it in the bag*, thought Terry. He looked down at his own empty page, bar the question he was yet to answer. 'What does orange mean to you?'

"Sod it," ejected Terry aloud. Another disapproving look from Maureen, but no one else seemed to have noticed. I'll just write whatever comes into my head, he decided. What do I think of when I hear the word orange?

He wrote a list:

- Orange juice
- Agent orange
- Was the fruit named after the colour or the colour named after the fruit?
- Holland
- Orange marches
- My aunt Edith's living room rug
- Lawrence's hair,
- Wotsits
- Garfield the cat
- Ernie from Sesame Street
- B & Q

- Goldfish
- errrrr...

Then he remembered what Doug, his boss at the Film Exchange, had once said to him after Terry and Lawrence had watched Stanley Kubrick's *A Clockwork Orange*.

"People say you can't rhyme the word orange. But I think you can."

He would have finished his speech there and then, if Terry hadn't asked him what did rhyme with orange.

"Minge," said a very proud and serious Doug.

I will write a poem, decided Terry.

A buzzer sounded to indicate that the one hour was complete. Contestants were asked to rip out what they needed from the pad and to hand the rest back in. The pads and pens were gathered in and an announcement was made that each finalist will be asked to the front of the stage to give their answer to the question in turn, alphabetically by first name. The winner would once again be decided by the audience via the Darius Global Research clap-o-meter.

Terry sat and listened to person after person give personal, emotive, and poignant responses. He liked Colin's answer about his mum's teeth being a golden orange due to years of saffron. Each answer was applauded loudly. Terry was starting to think he may well have misjudged the mood of the room.

Next up was Gareth Harper-Crouch. He looked confident. He cleared his throat and, in a surprisingly loud, deep and authoritative voice, orated his masterpiece.

"The word orange is both a noun and an adjective in the

English language. In both cases, it refers primarily to the orange fruit and the colour orange, but has many other associated meanings. The word is derived from a Dravidian language, and it passed through numerous other languages, including Sanskrit and Old French, before reaching the English language. The earliest uses of the word in English refer to the fruit, and the colour was later named after the fruit. Before the English-speaking world was exposed to the fruit, the colour was referred to as yellow-red."

On he went for five and half minutes. Explaining the origins of the word, the history of the word and, finally, he finished with a bold statement about the future of the word. That it would become extinct and replaced by ochre or tangerine.

The audience loved it. They lapped-up his knowledge and expertise. Terry was beginning to think giving it a pass on reading his answer aloud and a quick exit might be the best option.

He was encouraged by Sanjay's answer, though. He retold the time he and his brothers watched England versus Holland in the 1996 European championships at Wembley. Nothing showy or factual. Just a happy memory. There was polite applause from the crowd, but Terry thought he would be supportive and he clapped, too. The rest of the contestants looked around at him in amazement that he would conduct such a faux pas.

"And now Runner-up north-west division, contestant Terry Black."

Terry stood up and walked to the lectern. He tapped the microphone and made the speakers feedback a little. He looked down at his notes, then up at the waiting faces. Mostly people over fifty, sat down, stern-looking. It reminded him of Maureen from the south-west. He looked back at her. She, too, was scowling at Terry. She reminded him of his aunt Edith. There seemed to be a thousand Aunt Ediths glowering at him now. Every audience member was another Aunt Edith. Miserable, nasty, non-supportive Aunt Edith. Time to show her. Time to give her a reason to really be mad.

Terry licked his lips and started to read.

"There was a young man from Bolton..."

# WOLF MAN

An agitated man is walking toward a phone box. He is searching around his pockets, not really looking where he is going. The man reaches out to open the door and looks up. He is startled by a suspicious-looking man walking past nearby and nearly jumps out of his skin. He stands holding the door open, watching as the man ignores him and carries on his merry way, humming a little tune to himself, then he enters the phone box.

He picks up the receiver and notices wax on the earpiece. He wipes it on his sleeve with a disgusted look on his face. Fumbling in his jeans pocket, he pulls out some change and places it on top of the phone. From the other pocket, he produces a crumpled piece of paper with a phone number scrawled on it next to the words *Wolf Man*. He looks about to see if anyone is around. The rural road is empty, just like he hoped it would be. He puts all of his change atop of the phone, takes a coin and places it into the money slot. We hear the dialling tone, which rings several times, much to the impatience of the man. He drums his fingers against the window, runs his fingers through his hair, and again looks around outside. The man is getting increasingly nervous and annoyed.

"C'mon, c'mon. Answer the phone." After three or four more rings, it eventually stops. Someone has picked up on the other end.

"Hello...hello! Is that the Wolf Man?"

"Yes. This is the Wolf Man."

"Listen, pal, I paid you good money, and you've done a shitty job. I thought you were supposed to be good. I mean, you came highly recommended, but frankly, I'm pissed off." The angry rant is in stark contrast with the calm, low voice on the other end of the line.

"Hang on a minute, sir. What's your name?"

"Watts, S.P. Watts. You said you could do a good job. I'm supposed to pay you three grand and you—"

"And your address?" This seems to rile the man even more. He squeezes the phone tight in his hand, pressing his mouth right up against the handset.

"Look, you prick, you either come back and do the work properly or you ain't getting your money." There is a long pause before the calm voice speaks once more.

"Your address, sir?" The man feigns to smash the phone before taking a breath to calm himself.

"42A South Street."

"Let me check my file."

"Do that."

The man hears the sound of a phone being placed on a desk and again looks around outside. He can hear mumbling voices on the end of the line but cannot quite make out what they are saying, even though he tries hard. Listening intently, he closes his eyes. The more he concentrates, he thinks he can make out some words. He is in the room on the other end of the line. He can see this fabled

Wolf Man and whoever it is he's talking to. They stand in an office, facing each other, one giving the other a file, saying terrible things about him, saying how he won't pay, saying...

A loud banging makes the man start and drop the handset. He turns around to see a face at the window.

"Are you gonna be in there all day?" The man realises he has no idea how long this face has been listening to his conversation.

"Yeah. All day. Now piss off."

"Charming." The face moves away from the phone box, muttering under his breath. The man watches him move away. He picks up the headset and listens just in time to hear the calm voice return.

"Mister S.P. Watts, 42B South Street. Standard spouse job. Easy pay credit plan. Five percent deposit, pay the rest on..." Before he can finish, the man loses his cool once more and screams down the phone.

"It's A! A! 42A! You idiot."

"It says 42B in the file."

"Listen you to me, you, you listen to me. I come home from work to see police tape on my neighbor's door. What kind of moron..."

"The job is done."

"The hell it is! You get down here and kill my wife. I hired you to kill my wife. You came down to the wrong flat and cut my neighbour's wife's throat. That's no use to me. How the hell d'you think I feel? How is that supposed to make me feel?"

"As I said Mister Watts the job is done."

Incredulous, our man suddenly summons a newfound confidence.

"You're not gonna do it?" No reply.

"Well, I'm not gonna pay."

"You're not gonna pay?"

"No. So how about that then?" The man looks around for recognition of his new great plan, but he is still alone.

The voice of the Wolf Man has not changed since the start of the conversation and remains relaxed and in control. "You're not going to pay?"

"No, I'm not gonna pay. So sue me." He is pleased with this last line. He knows this nefarious Wolf Man won't be too keen on the law. The man laughs triumphantly.

Over the receiver, he again hears murmured voices. Then the Wolf Man returns. "And it's 42A South Street?"

"Yep. That's the one. Finally, he gets it right."

"Well, I'll be coming over real soon. Goodbye, Mister Watts."

The man listens to the sound of the dialling tone. He listens. The constant ring continues until he replaces the handset.

Outside the phone box, the face has returned. He taps on the window this time. The man turns around to face him, no longer so sure of himself. The face knocks on the glass again, even though they are making eye contact.

"Finished?"

# ANECHOIC CHAMBER

"Ever since the Robert Hook building was opened by Prince Charles in nineteen ninety-five, the facility has been used by a variety of acoustic engineers, sound theorists, and even musicians, including..."

The tour guide must have done this a million times. Clearly, she has no interest in what she is saying.

*You are supposed to enthuse your new employees, not bore them*, thought Clarissa. The research lab was state-of-the-art back then but is still considered the place to go to for all the people she mentions. *Doesn't sound that interesting, anyway. Who wants to study noise? Or not making any? Glad I'm just going to be working on the reception desk.*

The party of seven people is led by the guide around the four story building, room by room. Some they enter in and have a look around, some are off limits and people can only guess at what secrets may be inside.

Clarissa is distracted. Not just because she has no interest in acoustics, but because this morning she found out her girlfriend was cheating on her. Her cousin Michael had rung her to say he saw her with a man last night, and they were, as he put it, "exchanging spit" in the corner of the club. Clarissa told him it couldn't be Teddy, but then he sent a photograph. Well, four photographs, actually. From different angles. One where you can clearly see two people kissing and groping each other. And another where you can plainly see Teddy's face. It had come as a bolt out of the blue. She had no idea. Well, except that she was working late a lot, and her phone would ring and she would look at it, then go into the other room to take it, and she started wearing more dresses. Now, when Clarissa thinks about it, it was obvious. What a fool she'd been, ignoring the signs, sticking her head in the sand.

*I guess I just didn't want to think she'd done it again*, thought Clarissa.

"And this is my favourite area." The tour guide has suddenly perked up. It brings Clarissa out of her angry thoughts. She looks up to see where they are.

"This is our anechoic chamber." She pauses to let her audience take that in. Three or four smile and nod and look around at each other. They must have a clue what she's going on about.

"When we go inside, we will go in three or four at a time, no more." She then points in turn at her party. "You, you and you, come in with me first." She first points to blond guy, then curly girl, and Clarissa is the last.

"The rest of you stay outside with Leonard."

"Hello" A small bearded man gives an enthusiastic wave, even though he is standing but two feet away. The four of them go to enter a large metal door, but tour girl stops just at the entrance and points just above at a monitor.

"Security camera. Someone always needs to be outside

watching when someone is inside." She looks serious now, no longer smiling. They go inside.

The first thing Clarissa notices is that there is no floor. Well, there is a floor, but they are walking six feet above it on a net.

"Please, make sure nothing is loose in your pockets. You don't want to drop it through the net."

It's taught, but still bouncy, like a trampoline. The walls are all peculiar angles, shapes jutting out in all directions and, as Clarissa looks up, she notices the ceiling is the same.

"The room is designed so no echo or reverb is created. No sound exists once we shut the door." This is her dramatic cue to nod to Leonard, who has followed behind. He takes a step back outside and shuts the door on them.

"Now I want everyone to remember what my voice sounded like a moment ago. And listen to my voice now. No reverb. No bounce."

Everyone, even Clarissa, can hear the difference.

"Try and say a few words to each other."

"Hello."

"Hello."

Nobody is particularly inventive, and all are a little subdued by the sudden change in the tour guide and now their own voices.

"Now let's all keep silent for a whole minute." She holds up a finger and looks at her watch.

Everyone stays still. Not moving, not speaking. Not even sure where to look, they just stare at the angular walls. Clarissa's mind is not wandering. She does hear sound. She hears the sound of her own heart beating in her chest. She closes her eyes, listening inside herself. A sound joins the steady rhythm - she can only describe it as like standing on the bank next to the river near her house. It is her own blood being pumped around her body. This frightens her. She opens her eyes just as the tour guide drops her finger.

"One minute" The other two look at each other and smile. The tour guide looks at Clarissa. "What did you hear?"

"Erm. Me."

She seems pleased with this answer, and the others nod, too.

"Yes. It's so quiet, all you can hear is your own body working away. Amazing, isn't it?"

Blond guy suddenly finds his voice. "Hang on. For total silence, the door would have to be sealed, right?"

"That's right. Hence, the security camera and the person outside watching and timing."

"So how long before our oxygen runs out?"

"You could probably last around two hours if you regulated your breathing. But tests show that people can only last around forty-five minutes before they start to go a little crazy."

Blond guy does a spooky hand gesture towards the curly girl who lets out a little giggle.

"Okay, time for the other group to have a go." She puts a thumbs-up to the CCTV camera in the top left corner, and the door opens to reveal Leonard.

Clarissa waits outside with the other two and Leonard, who watches the monitor carefully while the others are inside taking their turn. Her thoughts turn once more to Teddy. She looks at the photographs on her phone. She doesn't cry. She is not upset, just angry. She puts the phone away. She looks up at the monitor. The tour guide bangs on the door. It makes no sound at all outside. A little snigger sneaks out of Leonard's mouth.

I wonder if Teddy would like to come visit me at my new job, thinks Clarissa. I could give her a tour, show her the anechoic chamber. Just need to find out if Leonard has a day off.

# SUMMER SONG

Andrew always wondered who named streets on housing estates. Was it the council? The building firm? Maybe they just go with a theme like names of trees and think 'that's brilliant!' Wouldn't it be great, he thought, if whoever it was had an imagination, or even a sense of humour, and named streets after 1970s TV shows or something obscure like Latin names for insects? No, he lives on a street that is part of an estate that has former presidents as their monicker. There are probably five or six estates named in a similar fashion all over the UK. What had Jefferson ever done for Leicester? And who has even heard of Hoover? Most people on our estate probably think it's named after the vacuum bloke. As he looks out onto the corner of the street from his flat window, Andrew can see the sign for Roosevelt Drive. The street is quiet. It is 3am.

Outside the row of connecting terraced homes is a clear glass phone box. Its light is the only illumination on the corner since the Baker kids shot the streetlight out with an air rifle. The filthy windows give it a warm, fuzzy glow and make it far more appealing than anyone who had smelled it would believe. There is a light coming from a bedroom window on the third floor of the house opposite. Andrew's bedroom window is also open. He can't sleep. It is far too warm, and he has no fan or any way of keeping cool.

Andrew moves back to his bed and lies atop of his sheets dressed only in his boxer shorts. He stares at the ceiling, wide awake, with his hands behind his head. He looks at the alarm clock on his bedside table; it reads 3:04am. He sighs and swallows dryly. He hears footsteps outside his window and tries to imagine who owns them. His curiosity gets the better of him and he labours over to his window. A long-haired youth walks by. He looks straight ahead of himself and seems to notice none of his surroundings.

Andrew watches him walk in and out of the light of the phone box until he disappears around the corner and he can hear the footsteps no more. He continues to stare out. Still no breeze from the open window. Still no let-up of the warm nights. He wishes the summers were shorter. This is the longest summer break ever. Classes don't start back at uni for another two weeks, and he has already finished whatever work he had for his cultural studies course. He could take his dad's advice and get a job. Well, a job that his dad approved of, as working part-time in a bar isn't a "real" job. A moment passes. Then, as clear as a record, he hears a voice sing. Quietly at first, then loud enough to be audible. Andrew looks around outside his flat. Still no one. The only place it could be coming from is the open window across the street. He listens, unsure if it is a recording or a real girl right there. He closes his eyes. The voice is enchanting; velvety, beautiful. It now dawns on him he cannot understand the words. Is that Urdu? It doesn't matter. The voice is soothing. He looks over at the house across the street again. The windows remain open, the light is still on, but there is no sign of anyone.

He listens intently, not even wanting to breathe in case he misses a note. He leans his head out of the window, wanting to get closer. The beautiful singing continues to enthral our man. He seems mesmerised until a smile fills his face, then runs downstairs, leaving his flat door wide open, and out onto the street barefoot. He stands below the window hoping to get a glance of the enchantress, the siren who has captured his soul. Standing in the middle of the road, in his boxers, staring up at the window. *Please keep singing*, he thinks, *don't stop*. He's jinxed it. The song comes to a natural end. He stays still, hoping it may start again. The light goes off. He squints his eyes, thinks he sees movement, but can't be sure.

Silence.

Morning, around 9:30am. Andrew is dressed and looks outside his window to see a middle-aged Asian man having a heated conversation in the phone box. Andrew goes outside, this time remembering to take his keys and lock his door. He walks over to the phone box and sits on the wall outside, waiting for the man to finish. Andrew stares up at the window that entertained him last night.

When the man eventually finishes his call, he comes straight out and the two strike up a conversation of friends.

"Why do we have to explain everything to the bloody council?"

"No idea, Mister Amir."

"Sorry, Andrew." Mr. Amir moves to one side, holding

the door open and gesturing for Andrew to go inside the phone box.

"No. It's you I wanted to talk to."

Mr. Amir raises a curious eyebrow and steps out of the phone box and lets the door shut behind him. "About what?"

Andrew starts to speak but falters and then smiles, embarrassed.

"Spit it out, lad. It can't be that bad. Can it?"

"No. It's just..." Mr Amir raises both bushy eyebrows, this time in anticipation. Andrew should have thought about what he was going to say first. Now he was thinking he might have imagined the whole scene.

"Did you hear singing last night?"

"Ahhh. Yes indeed, I certainly did." Andrew waits for a further explanation, but Mr. Amir starts to walk off in the direction of the house next door to Andrew.

"I think it was coming from the house opposite us. Your brother's house."

Mr. Amir stops. He turns to face Andrew. "That, my friend, is family. My niece."

"Your niece?"

"My eldest brother and his family are visiting. We are three brothers, Andrew. Aarif lives in Comilla. He is over with his wife and daughter for a month as it is our mother's seventieth. Did she wake you?"

"No. No, not at all. I thought perhaps I was delirious or something. What with the heat and half a bottle of white rum."

"It's the devil's piss. You shouldn't drink alcohol," Mr. Amir suddenly seems to get bored with the conversation and remembers he has more important things to be getting on with. "I'll see you later, Andrew." He walks into his house and shuts the door.

"Yeah, bye." Andrew takes a final look up at the window just in time to see the curtain suddenly pull shut.

After three hours or so intermittently looking through his window, Andrew goes for a walk. He strolls around the estate with no real intent or purpose other than to kill time and wonder if he should either ask Mr. Amir more about his niece, or go over and say hello to his brother, a 'welcome to the street' sort of thing.

For God's sake, he thought. She could be fifteen years old for all Andrew knew. So she has a lovely singing voice, so what? He walks into the newsagents and buys himself a chocolate bar. He walks back out, munching on his chocolate bar and thinking about the events of the previous night. Andrew continues daydreaming and mulling over his own blown-out-of-proportion problems, when he turns the corner and bumps into Mr. Amir.

"Watch where you're going, lad."

"Sorry."

Mr Amir picks up the cheque book Andrew has knocked out of his hand. As he does so, he reveals a young woman standing behind him. As Mr Amir rises back up, he notices Andrew looking over his shoulder.

"Oh. My niece, Aakarshika." She smiles at him, but does not speak. "But everyone calls her Shika."

"Hello." Andrew stays stock still, staring.

"I have a bill to pay, boy." Mr Amir gestures for Andrew to get out of his way.

"What? Oh yeah, sorry" He steps aside and Mr Amir strides on. Shika does not.

"Do you like music, Andrew?" she says.

"Did your uncle tell you?"

"Tell me what?"

"I thought..."

"Do you often stand in the street in your underwear, staring up at people's bedroom windows?"

"You saw?"

"Everything."

Andrew flushes.

"I'm glad you like my singing. Just remember, 'music is a magic beyond all we do here'."

Andrew smiles in awe.

"Is that an old Bangladeshi proverb or something?"

"J K Rowling, Harry Potter." With that, she smiles and follows her uncle.

Andrew watches as she glides past him. She seems to float rather than walk. He has it bad. Two weeks left of summer isn't enough. He wishes the summers were longer.

# CONDITION

They say it's so brave to talk about your mental health. But I find it easy. It's probably the most interesting thing about me. I'm schizophrenic. Schizoid. Crazy. Whatever you want to call it. The best thing to do is talk about it, mainly because people get the completely wrong idea of what it is. Remember that song football fans used to sing to goalkeeper Andy Goram? *"There's only two Andy Gorams."* Funny, yeah. Factual, no. Not sure why so many people think schizophrenia is multiple personality disorder. That can happen, but it is just one of so many symptoms. Films. They should take their fair share of the blame. So many sexy horror stories about nutcases with a good and bad side. Everyone loves an anti-hero. Everyone loves a good baddie.

Friend of mine at school called Chris had multiple personality disorder (or MPD if you like). Nine different personalities, he had. Nice guy Chris. Eight of them were slight variations on mood more than anything, but one... well, that was different. I remember ringing him up because he hadn't been in school for a whole week and his dad answered.

When I asked if I could speak to Chris, he just said, "Chris isn't here at the moment. It's Daniel, and he won't speak to you." Then, he said sorry and put the phone down.

Eight different versions called Chris, but the one who they didn't like had a different name. I guess it's easier to deal with if it's "not my son, some other kid." He came back to school after three weeks, didn't seem any different, but he thought he'd only been off a couple of days. Weird.

Me, my condition makes me have hallucinations. I'm not talking a palm tree oasis in a desert or some drug induced rainbow unicorn. Mine can be colours. Spiralling shapes, like a migraine, but without the blinding pain. But they can also be people. Fully formed, lucid figures in a room with me, talking but not to me, to each other. Not people I know. Not dead relatives, not ghosts, people I have never seen before. Living dreams, but I am fully awake. I feel like I could reach out and touch them, but I just watch. Even now, it takes me a moment to realise they are just apparitions. It's fine if I am on my own, at home. But if I am out and about, or if someone is with me, it can frighten them.

I used to get frightened as a child. I've always had them, you see, as far back as I can remember. My parents just thought they were imaginary friends until I was too old for imaginary friends. Then, the appointments started.

The reason I'm telling you all this is because...well, because I live in Norwich, and Norwich is the birth and burial place of Sir Thomas Browne. He is cited with the first ever usage of the word "hallucination," amongst other words such as "computer," "holocaust" and "suicide." Is it just a coincidence? Probably, but over eleven thousand people rang the mental health helpline in Norfolk in 2017. Maybe the lonely flat lands do something to people? All that open space. Nothing to do.

Sensory deprivation tanks were developed to help you be more aware of your senses. To feel, hear, smell, taste, see, think more clearly. Total darkness, total silence, and floating in a tank of water. Perhaps that's what rural areas are? Sensory deprivation zones. Maybe that's why so many of us have minds that wander, that create. Is boredom a great creator? "The devil makes work for...etc. etc."

What is meditation if it's not boredom? Doing nothing except thinking. I have no doubt Buddhists hallucinate. Is not the quest for Zen-like Satori a perfect place for hallucinations? The instructor usually informs the meditator to just ignore them and not get involved. They think of them as evil spirits, like a will-o'-the-wisp, attempting to lead you a stray off the path of enlightenment. Personally, I think they may help with enlightenment. I don't always hear what the hallucinations say, but they always seem to talk about things of importance, interesting, thought-provoking, maybe life changing things. Why not listen? Why not get involved?

You will have hallucinations at some point in your life. Does it mean you're crazy? Am I crazy? I'd like to think so, but really I'm just as sane as you, or you.

# THE LIST

"Here's the list."

"What list?"

"The list of everything you can't play."

"I thought I could choose my own playlists, as long as the station had it in stock."

"You can."

"So, what are you saying?"

"I'm saying these songs on the list are banned."

"That's censorship."

"Read it."

Evelyn scanned down the list written on a small piece of lined paper.

"Oh, right."

"Other than them, you can play anything else that is on the shelves."

"Hang on."

"What?"

"Most of these I get—*Knockin' on Heaven's Door* by Dylan, *Another One Bites the Dust* by Queen, *Staying Alive* by the Bee

Gees, but the Bay City Roller's *Bye Bye Baby* seems a bit over the top."

"It's the rules."

"And who makes these rules?"

"The hospital? Err...the NHS?"

"The NHS makes rules on what songs a hospital radio station should play?"

"I don't know. Just don't play anything on it."

"What about *Stairway to Heaven*? That's not on your list."

"If you think you have more you want to add to the list, you need to tell Warren first."

"I don't want to put more on, I just want to..."

"What?"

"Oh forget it."

She takes another look at the list in her hand. "Surely *That's Life* by Sinatra is a good thing?"

Gordon has already started walking away. Evelyn had only taken the voluntary job at Saint Cook's Hospital as a way of saying thank you. They had looked after her nan on the cancer ward before she finally stayed in the hospice. In and out for months on end with chemo and the nurses always made her nan laugh. Or was it the other way round? Yea, maybe it was the nurses that did all the chuckling with Nan. Never complained once. They adored her nan. And it also helped take her mind off her money worries.

"That was *Walking on Sunshine* by Katrina and the Waves, and that's all from me for today. I will hand you over to Gordon and the afternoon team."

Evelyn gave a little wave through the window of the soundproof booth, took off her headphones and grabbed her purse and went down to the coffee shop on the first floor to get her usual tea and Kit Kat, and have a natter with Halema.

"Thanks for the shout-out, Evie."

"No problem."

"Who was it again?"

"Hall and Oates."

"Never heard of them."

"Had some hits in the eighties."

"Are you allowed to play anything from this century?"

"I did offer to update the collection, but Warren is a little resistant to change."

"He is such a weirdo."

"He's okay. He's just set in his ways."

"I don't know how you cope working with those old men."

"Actually, I prefer it. They are more my pace."

"You're twenty-eight years old, girl. I am going to a party at that new club that's opened on Shaw Street, Friday night with Lucy from the pound shop, and you need to come."

"No thanks."

"Do you good."

"I'm trying not to spend any money."

"I know, I know. That's why you spend your weekend's playing records to sick people."

"The Kit Kat is my treat. As far as my budget goes at the moment."

"I'll take pictures and send them to you."

"Thanks."

Two customers were waiting patiently behind Evelyn. She sensed they were no longer so keen to wait while they chatted. Halema seemed incapable of multi-tasking, or rather, she didn't care. Customer service was way down her list of priorities. Evelyn thanked her friend and made her way back up the corridor to the elevator to get to the fifth floor. She had already planned to stay after her show to do some admin for Warren, who was away on a caravan trip with his wife and their two poodles.

Evelyn arrived at the double-sized lift that they had in most areas of the hospital and pressed the button to go up. She waited just a moment before the doors opened. The bell chimed, and she stepped inside. She was about to press the button marked five when she heard a voice shouting.

"Hold the door, please!"

Evelyn quickly pressed the door open button and waited for faces to appear. A squat orderly pushed an occupied bed towards the lift entrance.

"Thanks, love."

Evelyn let go of the button, and the doors closed behind the bed. "Which floor?"

"Five, please."

"Same as me."

The orderly nodded and then looked down at the patient in the bed and spoke in a rather loud and deliberate manner.

"Won't be long. Soon get you some proper pillows when we are on the ward."

Evelyn looked down, expecting to see someone elderly, but instead she saw a teenage boy. Bright blue eyes, and skin as pale as the surrounding sheets. He must have sensed Evelyn staring, for he turned and faced her. He gave her a huge smile. The kind of smile that can only evoke one response. Evelyn smiled back. The elevator exclaimed that they had reached their destination, and the orderly backed the bed out. Evelyn waited for them to be fully out, holding the door button once more.

"Thanks, love!" the orderly yelled-back once more to Evelyn. They seemed to be going the same way as her down the corridor, as she kept pace just a few steps behind, until they reached ward six and the orderly swung the bed around at an abrupt right-angle.

"Here we are!"

Evelyn decided to wait, as he had left only a small passage for her to get through while he swiped his ID card. It buzzed. He pushed the door. It did not open. He tried the card again, but still no luck.

"Oh for..."

He thought better of it. He banged on the closed door and waited. Nobody came. He was about to bang again, but then stopped himself and looked at Evelyn.

"Just do me a favour, love, and watch him while I get someone to open the door."

Evelyn went to answer, but he interjected before she could.

"I'll just be a minute." He jogged off back the way he came, leaving the bed stuck out across the corridor. As soon as the orderly was out of sight, a family with an elderly relative in a wheelchair came along.

"Can we get past, please?" said the man pushing the chair.

"Sorry."

Evelyn went round to the front of the bed and slid it up against the wall.

"Thank you," They carried on their way. Evelyn did one of those little smiles to show her acknowledgement.

"I don't think he's supposed to leave me, is he?"

Evelyn looked down at the boy. She shook her head. "He doesn't seem very bright. Keeps shouting for some reason. I think he might be deaf."

"I think he might be more used to patronising older people."

"Are you a doctor?"

"Me? No. I work in the radio station."

"Cool."

"Not really. Have a listen, and you will see how very uncool it is."

"Do you only play old stuff?"

"Old and naff."

"I like some old songs. My grandad was in a band. He taught me how to play guitar."

"Now that's cool."

"He was."

"Taught me how to play old rock songs from the sixties and seventies."

As he said this, he let out a small groan of pain and arched his back.

"Are you okay? Do you need me to get a nurse?"

"No. Once I'm in there, I can get some proper rest."

"Where is that idiot?"

He goes quiet for the first time. Evelyn looked at his smooth pale skin.

Suddenly, a face appeared at the ward door.

"Did someone knock?"

"Yes. This young chap is supposed to be with you."

"Lucas. I'm Lucas."

"Nice to meet you, Lucas."

The nurse looked at Evelyn.

"Where did you bring him from?"

"I didn't. I'm just baby-sitting."

"Baby-sitting! I'm sixteen."

"Well, let's get you in. Get the other end, please."

Just as Evelyn was about to help, a familiar shout came from the end of the corridor.

"I'm back. Cheers, love!"

The orderly skipped down toward them, his face pink and shiny. "It was my card. Needed a new one," he said between pants, trying hard to catch his breath. The nurse gave him a stern look.

"Get the other end."

Then he turned to thank Evelyn. "Thanks Miss...?"

"Evelyn."

She looked down at the boy and held out her hand and introduced herself again.

"Evelyn."

He could barely lift his arm and when she held his hand, it was cold and felt brittle and light, like a bird. She gently shook it just the once, not wanting to exert too much pressure on the tiny wrist. She looked at him again. He looked much younger than sixteen. There was nothing of him.

"Nice to meet you, Evelyn. Thanks for the baby-sitting." He said this last word in a mock-sarcastic way.

"Will you play me a song on the radio?"

"Of course, I'm on tomorrow morning. Anything in particular?"

"You decide."

And then the orderly and nurse pushed the bed into the ward and the door closed shut behind them.

As Evelyn walked up the corridor back to the radio station office, she was thinking of what song she could play for Lucas. She went to the archive cupboard, straight to the shelf marked sixties rock and pulled Led Zeppelin's fourth album off the shelf. She looked down the song list until she found the track she was looking for, *Stairway to Heaven*, and smiled.

# THE RED BALLOON

The red balloon snagged on the silver birch that sat at the back of a cottage garden. The gentle breeze that carried it there still blew, making it tremble as it seemed to struggle to free itself.

Alice opened her curtains and looked out of her bedroom window to see what weather awaited her on this Sunday morning. Grey skies again. *This must have been the shortest summer ever*, thought Alice. *Still, at least it isn't raining. Yet.* A jay bounced on to the lawn. First one of September that Alice had seen. She watched it look around, then fly up onto the fence post. Something seemed to catch its eye and scare it away.

"A visitor," Alice exclaimed to herself. A sixty-two year old widow who has lived on her own for over twenty years tends to speak to inanimate objects as well as to herself.

After putting on her wellington boots, Alice went out into the back garden. She looked up into the top of the tree. A red balloon with a long white ribbon was caught on a branch. Well, to be exact, it wasn't the balloon that was caught, or even the ribbon, but something attached to the bottom of the ribbon. But Alice couldn't quite see what it was from the ground.

"Stay there," she shouted up to the frightened balloon.

Alice turned and went to her shed. Inside, she moved a few boxes, buckets and brooms aside to reach her stepladder. She carried it out of the shed and down to the end of the garden, then leaned it against the trunk of the birch and shook it to make sure it was firmly secure. She looked up to where she needed to get to and then climbed the rungs.

Once on the top step, the breeze was stronger, so she hugged the tree to steady herself. Once she felt more assured, she looked across to the object she was trying to rescue. She decided she could reach it without stretching, so gripped the ladder with her right hand and slowly extended her left hand towards the ribbon. She could just about touch it with her fingertips. With two of her fingers, she clasped the ribbon. She squeezed as tightly as she could, then drew it towards her. Once she had enough ribbon, she grabbed it in a tight grip and easily freed it from the branch. She wrapped the ribbon around her left hand and started down the stepladder.

"Success. You're free my little friend." Alice intended to let the red balloon back on its way, up into the sky, free from the constraints of the tree in her garden, but then she looked at what was tied at the bottom of the ribbon. It was a square plastic sleeve and inside was a silver disc. She took the disc out of the sleeve. On one side was handwritten with a Sharpie pen, "Please, watch me."

The balloon rested on the ceiling of Alice's living room. She had taken the disc off the ribbon and given it a wipe down with a dry cloth. At first, she thought it was a compact disc, but with the message written on it, she decided to place it in the DVD player. She switched on her television and a menu page appeared on the screen. It was plain black with yellow text in the centre of the screen that simply said "play." Alice wondered what it could be. Why would someone send a disc away on a balloon? Was it some kind of message in a bottle to a Robinson Crusoe type figure stranded on a mountain? Was it a plea for help from someone kidnapped? A wish floated off by a child in a far off land? Her mind was reeling from all the possibilities. Alice pressed play.

Black Screen. Silence. Then a cut to a single armchair in a living room. A camera seemingly on a tripod was pointing straight on to an empty chair. Then some mumbling off camera. A thud and then someone angry and cross with themselves. The camera shook. It went out, then back into focus. A person walked into shot. They stood in front of the lens, but Alice could only see the legs and torso. Brown corduroy trousers, held up by a tatty leather belt around a slim waist. A blue button-down shirt with a black cardigan over the top. A hole in the left sleeve just above the cuff. The person seemed to be waiting for something. They rubbed their hands together. The right hand went into the trouser pocket. Alice wasn't sure whether or not they put something in it, but the hand came back out again empty. After what must have been two minutes, the person finally sat. A man, perhaps in his sixties. His hair was short and grey, one eyebrow was still dark brown and one had turned grey.

"If you have found me, well...hello." An uncertain smile, followed by a clearing of the throat. "My name is...actually my name isn't important. I just wanted to share something with you. Whoever you are. I am hoping this has found a home where you speak the same language as me, but I am uncertain how far my little red balloon would have carried me. Let's hope you understand." He rubbed his hands on his trousers, looked to the heavens, and paused to think. "Erm, where to begin?"

The doorbell chimes. Alice considered ignoring it but then paused the DVD player, leaving the old man frozen in thought.

"Parcel for Ms Whittaker?" Alice looked down at her feet. On her doorstep was a box. She leant down to pick it up. "Hang on. I need to take a picture of it for the records."

"Sorry."

The delivery man took a snap with his phone. "And one more for luck. Cheers." He turned, got in his white van, and sped away. Alice carried the parcel inside.

Back inside the living room, she placed the parcel on the coffee table with the painted on chess table that she had inherited from Aunt Ellen.

*Which to do first?* thought Alice. Open the parcel or continue watching the mysterious video? *Mustn't be distracted*, she decided, and pressed play once more.

"Shall I tell you where I was born? Is it important that you know who, or what I am?" He doesn't seem to have thought this through, thought Alice. "I think it's just important why I did this." He made a sweeping gesture, vaguely towards the camera. "I had to tell someone, so it looks like fate, and a strong wind, chose you. Who you tell is up to you.

"I am sixty-nine years old. Three months ago, I was diagnosed with pancreatic cancer. I've been having the usual, chemo and what have you..." He rubbed his very short grey hair. "Anyway, about three days ago, there was a ring of my doorbell and a delivery man was stood there with a parcel. I knew I hadn't ordered anything and I have no family—well, no one who talks to me, that is—so no one was sending me a package that I could think of. He leaves it on the doorstep and goes off on his merry way, and I take this package inside. It isn't heavy, and it's about the size of a shoe box."

Alice looked at the package on her coffee table. It wasn't very heavy, and it was about the size of a shoe box.

"I open it, and here's the thing, it was no wonder it wasn't heavy, because, like I said, I opened it and there was nothing inside. Well, there was tissue paper, which I rummaged through, but nothing else. I looked at the box. There was no return address on and the postmark was all smudged, so I couldn't read where it had been posted from. What a peculiar thing, eh?

"Well, I rang the post office, and they said it was sent private courier, but like I said, there was nothing on the parcel and nothing printed on the side of the van, as far as I can remember. So what to do? Well, nothing really. But then I got thinking about how nice it is to receive a mysterious package. When you've nothing going on in your life, that is, like me. It's exciting getting unknown parcels. Then, yesterday I decided to make this video and send it off, so that a random stranger would get a nice surprise. Nothing more, just a hello from a daft old man. I hope you liked it, and I hope you liked the way you got it. I did think about sending it to a random address through a courier, but this seemed to be even more...I don't know, it just seemed the right thing to do."

A melancholy smile briefly appeared on his face, followed by a sigh before he continued. "Now you have to decide what you want to do? Are you going to tell someone about this or keep it for yourself? Are you going to do something similar and send your own version of the mystery parcel? It doesn't matter what you decide. No pressure, but I'm glad I did it before I... well, you know." He paused, before seeming to decide that that was the end, and without a goodbye, he got up from his chair and walked towards the camera. His stomach covered the lens before it went black, before returning to the simple menu page.

Alice again looked down at the parcel in front of her. Surely a coincidence? Although she herself had not ordered anything online and no one that she knew had said they were sending her a parcel? She hesitated to open it, then walked over to the DVD player, took out the disc and replaced it in the plastic sleeve. She looked at the red balloon still resting on the ceiling. *There's a third choice. I could send this same message back out into the sky. Then someone else could find it and make a decision. Maybe they would have a parcel delivered to them?*

"Oh, stop being so bloody stupid." Alice decided she was just being silly, shook her head, and grabbed a pair of scissors to open the parcel. She ran the blade across the top of the box, and down the centre join where the tape held it together. She opened the box. White tissue paper. Alice laughed aloud, but it wasn't a very convincing laugh. She was nervous. She withdrew the pieces of tissue paper one by one, layer by layer. With every piece, she expected to see whatever was kept inside, until finally she came to the bottom of the brown box and all the tissue paper had been removed. She turned the box upside down and shook it. Nothing. She sifted through the crinkly paper all about her knees. Nothing. *How is this a good thing, silly old man?* Alice threw the box on the floor.

Alice had always loved to live on her own, but now she was afraid. The beautiful scenic countryside, living so far from anyone else in a cottage, had always been her ideal, but suddenly she felt vulnerable. She sat and listened. Silence. Once again, Alice gathered herself.

"Now who's being silly, Alice?" She scrunched the tissue paper up into a ball and put it back in the empty box. She took the box into the kitchen and threw it in her recycling bin, then grabbed the kettle, filled it with water and switched it on. "A cup of tea solves all of life's ills." She went back into the living room and clasped the ribbon attached to the balloon. "And you, my little friend, can go in the bin as well." Taking the scissors from the coffee table in one hand, the balloon in the other, she braced herself for the loud bang. She held it for a moment, then looked at the blank television screen. She looked back at the balloon. The scissors dropped to her side. "Option three it is, then."

Alice walked outside to her garden with the plastic sleeve tied back onto the ribbon. The wind had picked up from earlier. She stood away from the trees and let go. The red balloon floated high, carried by a gust out towards Logan Forest toward town.

"I wonder if it will land there or carry on?" Alice pondered the red balloon's future for a second. "Goodbye, red balloon."

After making herself a cup of tea, she sat down and picked up the book she had been reading (an old-fashioned mystery about a murder on a seaplane) and settled down.

"Well, he was right about one thing. It does make the day more exciting." This time, Alice managed a more genuine laugh. She had only read around two pages when the doorbell went again.

# THE SAVOY

"No, Mum. I will, Mum. Uncle Peter has it. Okay. Yeah, okay. I'll call you next Tuesday about the same time. Yeah, you too."

Ash put down his mobile phone and turned the volume back up on the television. He was watching a DVD of a film he had probably watched over fifty times. These old favourites were his comfort blanket. It had been three weeks since he started his new job, moved out of the family home and into his first flat. His mum worried about her youngest child anyway, but his first job after university was in a totally different country. It was actually only eighty miles down the road from his parent's house in Clyro, but it was indeed across the border of Wales into England.

His mother worried about him being a teacher in a secondary school, and his father didn't trust the English. But Bristol had far more going on than the sleepy village of his childhood. Ash hadn't seen any of this exciting city life just yet, as he was still finding his feet. He had made a friend at work but had not been invited out socially yet. He looked at his phone again and contemplated ringing some old pals back home but had a sudden bout of bravery, or possibly shame, and decided against it. *Time to get out and have an adventure*, he said to himself. *But first I need to finish my film. Tomorrow is Saturday.* It was much better to go out discovering in the daytime rather than after nine o'clock at night, Ash decided.

After a shower and breakfast of orange juice, coffee, and toast with his mum's home-made marmalade, he tidied his Empire magazines away and realised he was just delaying. After a deep breath, he decided to stop being such a small-town boy and bite the bullet. He strapped on his shoes and stepped out of the door.

It was pretty busy even at 8am on a weekend morning by the quays. Places were opening and people were busying themselves in their purposeful lives. Ash wandered along the streets saying good morning to people. Some returned the greeting, some just looked at him strangely and grunted. *There are some nice-looking cafés*, he thought. *After a while of looking around, I shall sit at a table outside, order a coffee and a Danish and sit and watch people.* Not an amazing leap into the unknown, but a plan of action, at least. After around twenty minutes of casually walking with his hands in his pockets, he came across a second-hand bookstore that was pulling up its shutters.

"Morning," said Ash to the grey-haired man in a deep purple T-shirt who seemed to be the owner. He turned and looked at Ash, smiled, and nodded.

"We're open. Go in if you like?"

"Thanks."

Ash went through the tatty mahogany door, and a reassuring bell gently tinkled. It was much smaller than it looked on the outside. Well, not smaller because there was so much in it, but there was very little room to move. Book upon book in seemingly random stacks adorned everywhere he looked. A narrow track weaved its way through the forest of words, wide enough for a grown man's foot to stand lengthwise, but nothing more. Ash carefully stepped along the pathway.

On closer inspection, the books were piled into categories, some by genre, others collected by the same author. There was some kind of method to the madness. He shut the door behind him, and the bell rang again. Then he breathed in the smell. So many old books, many leather bound, lots tattered and torn, but all with that smoky, earthen musk. *Had to be up there with the smell of fresh roasted coffee and Jenkin's bakers first thing in the morning*, thought Ash. He looked upwards and saw the stacks reached all the way to the ceiling, with almost no gaps. *How could anything be found in here?* he thought. But maybe that was the point. Perhaps they were not meant to be sold. Another ding from the door.

"If you're searching for something in particular, let me know and I can show you where to look."

"I'm just looking."

"Most people do."

Ash didn't want to be most people.

"Do you have any cinema-related books?"

"Round the corner to your left, about halfway up, near the picture of Sophia Loren."

Ash nodded and proceeded slowly in the vague direction of the bookshop owner's finger. As he edged past the corner, he saw the photograph of the Italian screen goddess and made his way over.

There was one long mound of biographies from Bogart to Jack Warner. At least six copies of Hollywood Babylon and to the left of these lots of published screenplays. Ash turned his head on its side and moved up the pillar of scripts. Plenty of films he recognised, and some he didn't.

"Any hardback is five quid. Paperbacks are two."

Ash looked around expecting to see the owner looking at him, but he was busy rearranging. He continued to search. As he got higher, it became difficult to see the spines. Once again, as if reading his mind, the owner spoke.

"I've got a ladder for the top ones."

"That's okay."

"Not a problem if you change your mind."

He had still not looked at Ash.

"If you like films, you should go to the cinema."

*Well, why I hadn't I had that brainwave?* thought Ash. "I do go to the cinema, thanks."

"Not that hideous multi-screen crap-house. They don't like films, and they're only interested in selling popcorn to idiot teenagers. I mean The Savoy."

"The Savoy?"

"Talbot Street. I'll draw you a map."

"If you've got the post code, I can use my phone."

"I'll draw you a map."

Ash nodded. The bookshop owner grabbed a ledger from under a pile of newspapers and took the pencil that was behind his ear. He did that thing Ash had only seen in black and white films; he licked the end of the pencil before writing. When he had finished scribbling, he finally looked at Ash. Handing him the scrap, he spoke.

"They should be open today."

"Thanks."

Ash took the paper. There was a circle with Carson Books written next to it and an arrow that zigzagged through a few streets before coming to another circle labelled Savoy.

"Easy to find, if you have a good map. But some of them streets are just cobbled back-alleys so your GPS bollocks would send you the long way round at best."

"I appreciate the tip. I've not been in town long."

The man smiled, revealing his left-sided front tooth was missing. "I'd never have guessed." Then he belly-laughed at his amazingly funny joke.

Ash smiled back and made his way to the door. All the while being laughed at along the way. He got to the door, opened it to hear the now familiar bell and was about to exit when the man abruptly stopped laughing.

"You'll have to pay cash. They don't have a machine."

"I'll do that. Thank you."

Ash checked his wallet. Inside was a twenty-pound note and some loose change. Plenty, he thought. He took a look at the map, turned it around so the bookshop was at the bottom, and scanned around himself. There was a knock on the window behind him. He turned to see the bookshop owner pointing in the direction he should start. Ash pointed his finger in the same way as if to ask a question. The man nodded in an exasperated manner, shook his head, then went away from the window. Ash followed the map.

After a couple of wrong turns, a dead end and bumping into a woman carrying a bucket of fish, he arrived at what he thought should be the location on the map. He looked around him. To his left was a row of terraced buildings that were empty and boarded-up. To his right were the backs of shops, yards with various security measures depending on the store. Nothing behind him. In front of him was a three-storey-high building. It had double doors at the front with four steps leading up to them, no upstairs windows, a sign above the door that said "SVOY" with a gap in between the S and the V. Next to the double doors on the right was a billboard. As Ash moved closer, he looked at the poster in the glass casing. "Ray Harryhausen double-bill" was emblazoned across the top with pictures of two *Sinbad* films underneath. He loved these old adventure movies, and his dad had told him all about the master animator many times when he was young.

This could be my lucky day, decided Ash. He stepped up to the heavy wooden doors and creaked one open.

He stepped inside to a darkened foyer. He closed the door behind him and stood a moment to let his eyes adjust. Classic deep scarlet carpet, posters on the walls, and over there the box office. A small booth was on one side of the foyer, next to some stairs. There was no one on the counter, but there was a bell.

"Hello?"

Nothing.

"Hello?"

Then an elderly woman with white hair, green nylon dress, dark-rimmed spectacles and an eyepatch over her left eye came out from a door at the side behind the counter.

"There's a bell, right there." She didn't point to it, but she seemed irritated.

"Oh yes. Sorry."

"Well?"

"Has the film started, as I can't see any times anywhere?"

"Not yet."

"Great. One adult ticket, please."

"Four pound."

Wow, thought Ash, just four quid for two classic films. He gave her the twenty. She didn't seem very happy about that, either.

"Nothing smaller?"

"Sorry, no."

A big sigh. Then, she opened a drawer under the counter and counted out sixteen pound coins. Ash slid them into his hand and into his trouser pocket. Then she handed him a ticket.

"Which one is on first?"

"Eh?"

"Is it Seventh Voyage or Golden Voyage?"

"What you on about?"

"The Sinbad double bill?"

She just stared at him with a confused look on her face.

"The poster outside said—"

"Oh, that's not been changed for six years."

"So what did I just buy a ticket for?"

"The film."

"I know, but which one?"

"How do I know? I just sell the tickets."

Pointless asking for my money back, thought Ash. I may as well see what is on. "Is it up the stairs?" Ash pointed in the direction of the stairs right next to them. She followed his finger, sighed, then slowly nodded. She then disappeared back through the door she came from.

"I'll take that as a yes."

He walked up three flights to two more double doors. As he arrived at the top step, someone stepped out of the shadows.

"Tickets, please."

"Oh yes, sure."

Ash got the ticket back out of his pocket and went to hand it over. It was then he noticed it was the same woman from the box office downstairs.

"Oh, hello again."

She gave him another confused look, took his ticket and punched a hole in it.

"Sit anywhere you like."

"Thanks."

She disappeared again. I am sure that patch was on the left eye downstairs, mused Ash. He walked through the double doors.

Inside was a decent-sized auditorium with around two-hundred seats. Not one of them was filled. He was the only person here. On the screen was a holding page displaying the words "safety curtain" and disco versions of John Williams tunes were being piped quietly through the speakers. Ash sat middle row, middle seat. He took out his phone and set it to airplane mode.

Ash looked at his watch. He had been sat for around ten minutes. Nothing had happened. No film, and no one else had arrived. He looked behind him at the projection window. A small white light was visible but nothing else. Then Ash felt the hand on his shoulder.

"Jesus!"

"Sorry, didn't mean to frighten you."

A man with the most complicated comb-over Ash had ever seen adjusted his thick glasses before smiling.

"Alan, the projectionist."

"Right?"

"Well, it's a bit awkward…"

"What is?"

"Just had the manager on the phone and he says I can't run the film unless there are at least three people here."

"Oh."

"Clearly, you'll get a refund. No problem there."

"What film was it?"

"Sorry?"

"What film?"

"Oh yes, an Italian drama, The Seven Valleys."

"Sounds good."

He shrugged non-committally. Ash was disappointed not to be seeing the *Sinbad* films but quite liked the sound of this new film.

"If I was to pay for three tickets, that would be the same, wouldn't it?"

"Errrm?"

"Technically, there are three people here: me, you and the lady in the box office"

"Hilary."

"Yes, Hilary."

Ash pulled out another eight coins from his pocket and placed them in Alan's hands.

"Oh, I see. You'd be right there. I'll drop this off with Hilary and get back to my office." He turned to go, but then thought better of it.

"Tell you what, I won't bother with the trailers and adverts, as it's only you."

"Great."

"Let's get this show on the road." He snorted a laugh and went on his way.

In just a few moments, the BBFC title card appeared, the lights dimmed, and the film began.

~

Stepping out into the daylight, Ash's stomach rumbled. He checked his watch, lunch time, so decided to find his way back to one of these cafés he had liked the look of this morning and get himself something to eat. He looked back at The Savoy. *How the hell did that stay open?* he thought.

He took out the map, turned it upside down and weaved his way back to the busy streets of the town centre. Arriving back at his point of departure, he decided to go back and thank the bookshop owner. He was feeling a little more confident and determined that the eccentric people he encountered today could be his new friends. He entered the shop. It seemed to be empty, before a face appeared from behind a mound of novels.

"With you in a minute."

Again, he didn't look in the direction of his customer. Ash waited by the door. In a moment's time, the bookshop owner came over.

"Any hardback is five quid. Paperbacks are two."

"Yes, I know. I came back to say thanks for the tip about the cinema."

"Cinema?"

"The Savoy."

Nothing. A nervous pause from Ash. The bookshop owner stared through him, as if he had never seen him before.

"I don't know any cinema. The Savoy burned down years ago."

Ash started to get the map out.

"You drew…"

Then that same loud laugh permeated the shop.

"Had you going there, lad. Your face was a picture."

"Very funny."

"Glad you liked it. He's all right is Alan."

"Yes, I just wanted to say thank you."

He stopped laughing and raised his eyebrows. And slowed down.

"Did you now? Did you?" He smiled and then held out his hand. "Carson Moore."

"Ash, Ash Helfer." They shook hands.

"Wait there a second."

He turned and went around the corner to the left. Ash heard books being moved and Carson shouting back as he searched for something.

"I remembered it after you'd gone. Here it is." He re-emerged holding a paperback. He handed it to Ash, who read the title aloud.

"Italian Neorealism."

"Thought it might be useful."

Ash pulled out two pound coins from his pocket and handed them to Carson.

"Two for a paperback?"

"That's right."

"Thank you."

"Have a good one."

With that Carson gave Ash a friendly slap on the shoulder, turned and went about his business with a cheery whistle.

Ash ordered a cheese and tomato toastie and a cup of very appropriate Italian roasted coffee. He sat and searched through the appendix of his new book looking for the *Seven Valleys* or *Sette Valli* but couldn't see it anywhere. He got out his phone and googled it. No films with that title. The only references were to a religious story, that *The Seven Valleys* was a guide for human conduct, that one should search out one's "own imperfections and not think of the imperfections of anybody else." This was not Ash's strong point. Both his parents were lapsed Church of England. He could ask Mrs Wurther, the Religious Studies teacher at school on Monday, but then again, he might not.

She seemed a little scary.

# THE DEARLY DEPARTED

"He was a great bloke, your dad."

I nod as the ruddy-cheeked man before me shakes my hand. He was one of several people who I had no idea of who they were. Various old timers dressed in black. Paying their respects to good old Daryl.

"Your brother told some good stories up there, you know, at the service."

I smile a quick acknowledgement. He seems to be on his own.

"Larry, by the way."

He shakes my hand again.

"And how did you know dad?"

"Worked together thirty odd years ago. Shearings Financial Holdings. Me and him were sales reps together. Had a right laugh, always the joker, your old man."

"He was."

"Do you know Cyril?"

"Can't say that I do."

"He passed on last year. Always wore a wig?"

"No idea."

"He worked with us for a couple of years before he set up on his own."

I try to look interested. He doesn't seem to have anyone else to talk to and, to be honest, I don't want to talk to anyone anyway. I am quite happy for Larry to reminisce at me.

"Thought your dad might have mentioned Cyril."

"He didn't."

It seems I have scuppered that anecdote. He looks over both shoulders, one after the other, as if he is about to tell me a big secret, and leans in slightly. In a slightly lower voice, he simply exclaims, "This must have cost a few quid?"

I don't really know what to say, so he continues with a sweeping finger pointed in the general area of the room. "This lot. Buffet, drinks!"

He holds up his glass.

"Lots of people here as well. Well liked, your dad. Great bloke."

He bites his lip in thought, then suddenly smiles, remembering a new story to tell.

"He ever tell you about the time he broke his finger?"

"He had a few stories he used to tell us. I remember a broken leg when he fell off the back of a bus."

"Yeah, that was a good one. No, this was me and him."

"No, then."

And then he has me. And I am happy he does. No one else seems to want to interrupt until we have finished and I don't have it in me to speak to family. Larry and his stories are much easier to deal with.

"We had just done a re-mortgage deal with some shop owner in Timperley. Back then, we would go out in pairs and take turns driving. Daryl drove that day, that yellow

Cortina he had. Do you remember it never used to start on cold days?"

This I do remember. Dad's car was notoriously unreliable in the winter. If we hadn't had lived on a hill, he would have never have gotten to work. Always jump-starting it down the slope to get it going. When we were a little older, me and my brother would help push it. We didn't need to help as gravity was perfectly capable of managing on its own, but it made us feel like we were useful and we got to wave him off as he pulled away.

"We were coming back to the office with the signed papers, and we pass Talbot Park. You know the fields they have on the far side? Well, there's a group of kids playing football and your dad turns to me and says — 'fancy a game?'"

He chuckles, a throaty smoker's rattle.

"Like that, your dad. So we park up, take off our suit jackets and give these kids a shout. It was all right to talk with strangers back then. Nobody thought you were up to no good like they do nowadays."

He looks serious for a moment before seeming to remember the point of his story and carrying on.

"All different sizes and ages these kids, about a dozen of them, just kicking a tatty old caser around the park, shirts down as goalposts, and what have you. Your dad says we'll be goalies, one for each team. The kids agree and off we go. I let in a couple of goals for the little ones, you know, but your dad was pulling off some great saves. Diving here, there and everywhere. He wasn't afraid to take the kids' legs out from under them as well. Made sure nothing got past him. Pretty bloody agile for a big bloke. Anyway, this bigger kid, you know the sort, chunky, taller than the rest, probably his ball. He's on my team, and he's getting a bit naffed off with your dad, as his team was winning before we showed up. So he decides he's not gonna pass the ball to his teammates, and he's gonna take control of the situation and score himself. Off on a run he goes. Knocks a couple of the smaller kids out of his way, bears down on goal, but your dad is waiting, primed, ready to spring like a cat. The kid winds up his right foot and blam!"

He pauses like any good storyteller.

"This kid catches it sweet. You know when you just hit it on the sweet spot and it flies like an arrow?"

I nod in agreement.

"Bobby Charlton couldn't have hit it any harder. Whoosh!"

He even mimics a right-footed kick as he says it.

"Your dad gets to it. Stops it. But it hits him right on the end of his index finger. Right on the tip and pushes it into his hand. He screams out in pain, hits the floor like a sack a spuds. Fat kid carries on running, picks up the loose ball, rounds your dad, who is on the grass in agony, and slots it home. Not content with the goal, he proceeds to dance around your dad with a victory celebration Lee Sharpe would be proud of. Well me, I was in tears laughing at the other end of the pitch."

He smiles broadly, and I can't help but smile, too.

"I had to drive back to the office. We strapped his fingers up with some sticky tape and a lolly stick and told Cyril he fell over leaving the shop after the deal. We had a right laugh in them days. I could tell your some stories about your dad."

"If I had known you were coming, I would have asked you to tell some of these at the service."

"Oh, I couldn't have done that. Your brother did a good job."

Larry seems like a really decent man. He seemed to have lots of fond recollections of dad.

"The story about the toothache was a good one that your brother told. I bet you've got lots of great stories, too."

"Only the ones he told us. Great stories about himself. That was a great story you just told me, Larry. I had never heard it before. I never knew he could kick a football. I knew he liked to watch it, but he never once took me and my brother to a park and kicked a ball around. Not once."

Larry looks awkward. He shifts about in his ill-fitting grey suit.

"It was nice to meet you, Larry. Do you know anyone else here?"

He just shakes his head, silent now, not knowing what to say.

"Come on, I'll introduce you to some other old friends of his. They will love your stories."

"I didn't mean to..."

"Larry." I stop, take his arm and look him straight in the eyes. I smile a genuine, warm smile. He hasn't upset me or brought back painful childhood memories. I really did enjoy his story and liked meeting such a kind-hearted soul. "Thank you."

"Oh, yeah, right."

He nervously smiles back, and we continue over to a group of three other old gents who also have nothing but good things to say about my dad.

# ACKNOWLEDGMENTS

Edited by Pam Elise Harris at
www.kitchensinkedits.wordpress.com

Cover Illustrations by Jonny Lindsey @paint_yer_brain
Jonnylindsey89@icloud.com

Proofread and formatted by Paul Draper at
www.theblackgate.co.uk

Thanks to Juliet, Harris and Louis
and to Paul Draper for all his assistance.

# ABOUT THE AUTHOR

Stephen is married with two sons and is a University
Lecturer in Film Production. He has written and directed
several short films and a feature.
This his first book of short stories.

Stephen's Amazon Author page is at:
www.amazon.co.uk/Stephen-Murphy/e/B00ACHD9IQ

Printed in Great Britain
by Amazon